Damaged Love

&

Forever Bound

Book Two in the Bound Series

by

Layla Stevens

Damaged Love and Forever Bound

Published by: Scilicet Group LLC

4139 South Nolan Drive

Pearland, TX 77584

ISBN – 978-1-941839-03-4

Cover Design by: Rachel A Olsen

then delete it from your system, and destroy all copies.
Thank you.

Dedication

To all the people who have been adopted — especially my daughter Sage Bullock. I did not give birth to you, but my heart chose you. You have been my light since I first met you. I love you more today than I did yesterday, and I will love you more tomorrow than today. Have faith in yourself baby, because you are so worth believing in.

I will always love you!

Love,

Mom

Acknowledgements

Patrice Krumm: Thank you from the bottom of my heart. Your friendship means the world to me. You truly are *one in a million*, and I would not trade you for all the *pink* in the world.

Lynn Palmer: Thank you for all you do for me.

To my Kick Ass Street Team: I love you with all the pink sparkles in the world.

To my Family: Thank you for believing in me.

To my amazing Beta Readers: Candice Burna Tice, Amy Abendroth, Jenni Crawford, Jenn Marie Lopez, Stephanie Nett, Laura Soask {Tolbert}, and all who helped in this journey.

To my Proofreader: Jenni Crawford may there always be too many commas in all my books. I will always add extras just for you

To my Mom: Thank you for giving me the love of reading when I was younger. It has inspired me to become who I am today.

And to my amazing daughter Sage: Thank you for being my number one fan. I love you gumdrops and popsicles & all the sketti and meatballs in the world.

TABLE OF CONTENTS

PROLOGUE

Damaged

"I'll never stop dreaming that one day we can be a real family, together, all of us laughing and talking, loving and understanding, not looking at the past but only to the future."

~LaToya Jackson

The moment Millie and Seth walk into my room, Garrett narrows his eyes. I glare at them and grind my teeth.

"What the fuck do you want? Why are you here?" I snap, "Why now? Haven't you hurt me enough over the years? You have some nerve coming in here."

"Kayla, we're sorry for everything," Seth apologizes, appearing sincere.

The majority of the time he is put together—hair slicked back, but today he looks like a mess. The dark brown bags under his eyes are quite prominent, and I can see his face is bruised and has several cuts. Wow! He took a beating. I can't help but laugh under my breath because whoever did it needs a damn medal.

"You say you're sorry, but what about the past? What about the years your boys abused me, and then you treated me like shit?" I suck in my lip before continuing, "The fact they raped me, and you never did anything. Then, when I finally get the nerve to tell you, you basically just push me under the fucking rug like I didn't exist. Well guess what—I do exist. You were my parents. You were supposed to protect me. What did I ever do to you to make you not love me?" I whack the mattress of the bed with my right hand and wipe a tear with my left hand. "What kind of monsters are you?"

"They came here to answer that question. It's time to open your ears and heart and shut down your mind," Patrice taps my hands. "I know you're angry Kayla, but you can't hold onto the anger any longer. Let her explain, and then if you want to be mad, that will be fine. Hell, I will even be mad with you, but right now give her a chance to explain."

I jerk my hand from hers and scream, "You're on their side? Out of all the people who would take their side, you can't be that person. Please don't be on their side!" I feel her take my hand just like a mother would.

"Kayla, I'm not on their side, I'm always on your side, but you need to hear some of the things Millie has to say," Patrice stares at Millie and directs, "You may continue, but just know this is the time for you to tell her the truth. No half-assed answers."

"Okay, Dr. Doyle, I have no reason to lie any longer. All of my skeletons are now out, so she may as well know them too. We all have our own secretes—don't we, Dr. Doyle?"

"I don't know what you are talking about Millie," I say to her and a chill runs down my spine.

"Kayla, I was never a good mom. Hell, I didn't even know how to be a mom. My mother was never there, and I was an only child. I never had anyone to help me," she wipes a tear from her face and continues on about her life in a run-down trailer that never had any heat and her starvation that was so bad; the only meal she ever ate was the free meals at school. How she never got new clothes and never had anything but a raging alcoholic mother who spent more time at the bar than at home.

"I had known of Seth from school. He lived in a nice neighborhood that I always walked past when heading home. He lived on the right side of the city. I always told myself one day I would be someone, and I would live in a house that was so grand and beautiful that people would envy me. I got that the day I ran into Seth in the hallway of St. Roman Catholic School in Charleston, South Carolina. He was tall, lean, and muscular. He was shorter than most of the guys in school, but he never let them intimidate him. He always had this look of 'I know I am someone'. Seth had on his letterman's jacket he got from being on the wrestling team. He was damn good too."

"I remember gazing at him so intensely and wishing he would be my knight in shining armor and he was. I had been so happy when he bent down to help me pick up the papers that slipped out of my hand. I just knew he would laugh at me like all the other kids, but he didn't. He picked them up and handed them to me, and we made small talk. He asked my name, and I told him it was Millie. He thought I said Tillie, and I had to correct him. He said, 'I know, I was just kidding with you.' and laughed."

"I was never pretty—more like the ugly duckling. I had stringy, reddish-blonde hair, lots of freckles, and I was not skinny. I had curves and lots of them. I was what you now call a plus sized girl. Over the next few weeks he would walk me to class and talk to me in the hallways. I loved being around him. One day he asked if he could take me home. I did not want him to know where I lived, so I told him no. But of course he's a hard-headed man and wouldn't take no for an answer."

"On the way home, I tried my best to convince him to just drop me off, even went as far as trying to open the door of his jeep to just jump out. But he pulled over and took my hands as I was crying and told me whatever it was that I was trying to hide, he could handle it. I wiped the tears that were flowing down my face and told him where I lived. He pulled up to the rusted old mobile home that had busted windows and a rotted out wood porch. I was embarrassed. No one had ever seen my home. I had never brought anyone here, nor would I want to. This place was horrible, nothing but bad memories. Seth kissed my hand and told me to wait. He got out of the jeep, walked around, and opened my door for me. I remember calling him a gentleman.

"He told me I was more than where I live. That even though I didn't have a fancy house, it didn't mean I was worthless. I still didn't want him to see my house. It was so embarrassing, and what if my mom was home? Odds were that she was at the tavern, bar stool number three. It's the place she really called home.

"We went inside, but the lights wouldn't turn on. Seth was so upset that I didn't have power or heat.

He refused to let me stay in the cold, promising to take care of me.

"So I jumped at the chance. Little did he know, I was pregnant by Jason Woodrow. I never mentioned the night Jason and I got together. It was a mistake, and he would never admit to anyone that he slept with a girl like me. I was a little over six weeks pregnant at that point. So I still had time to play it off. I went home with Seth that night and never looked back."

My mouth dropped. I must have looked like a large mouth bass.

"Kayla, close your mouth. The one thing I did right was teaching you to be a lady. You had all of those charm classes, and I know you have manners. Use them. At any rate, I married Seth at a small local wedding chapel across the state line. We left South Carolina in the dust, and we drove until we got to Seattle. I have many faults, Kayla. I married a man even though I knew he was a womanizer. I let him believe that Edwin and Elijah were his kids. I have faults, and I'm okay with them. Now I've told you my story, and I hope that when Edwin and Elijah wake up we can all sit down and talk about everything. I am truly sorry, Kayla, about your childhood. I hope that you can forgive me one day."

I look over to Seth. I see a man that has aged. For the first time in his life, he looks tired and worn out, like he's lost his will to live. But Millie still looks like a freaking model. You can see the worry in her face, but it's distant. She has the look of a woman who never shows emotion. I use the term *stone cold*. She would make any prisoner admit what crimes they have done.

"Does this woman ever show any signs of remorse?" I think to myself.

Officer Jernigan strolls in.

"Kayla."

"What is going on?" I nervously scratched the top of my hand.

"I've come to tell you that Edwin and Elijah are..."

CHAPTER ONE

Who Lives and Who Dies

"My family is my strength and my weakness."

~Aishwarya Rai Bachchan

Officer Jernigan strolls in. "Kayla."

"What's going on?" I nervously scratched the top of my hand.

"I've come to tell you that Edwin and Elijah are..."

"Well spit it out. Officer Jernigan, they are what?"

"Well I hate to say this, we lost Edwin. The doctors did all they could, but he was too damaged. His heart could not take the drugs that were in his system. There was no way to save him. They tried everything they could, but there was nothing else they could do."

I hear Millie scream and start sobbing.

"Elijah is still touch and go. Right now he's in a medically induced coma. It's safer for him."

The shrieking and screams from Millie tear me apart.

I stutter, "I'm so sorry Millie, but he was going to kill me and Violet. I know my words will never bring him back."

"Kayla, you killed my son," bitterness and anger color Millie's voice, "I will never forgive you for this. You are dead to me, Kayla. You should have stayed gone and never come back. We were all better off without your stupid ass."

"Now, Millie don't be so dramatic," Seth states. "She was protecting herself from your sons. What did you expect her to do? Let them rape her all over again? We should have done something years ago. Maybe then they wouldn't have turned out the way they did. They didn't have the best childhood either. They had us, but we were never really parents. We were always too self-involved. I was always chasing a skirt, and well, you were doing whatever it is that you do. Frankly, I have no idea what it is you do all day long."

"I don't give a rat's ass what she was doing. My son is dead. How the hell are you so God damned calm and collected Seth? Our son is dead. D. E. A. D. What part of that don't you get? He is not waking up. And as far as me doing stuff all day long, I take care of our house and make sure that your whores are paid for."

"I get it Millie, but as you just said, the boys were not and are not mine. So excuse me for a minute if I am not kissing your ass."

"Officer Jernigan, thank you for telling us, what happens now?" I ask.

"There will be an official investigation, Kayla, so don't leave Seattle. And don't make me come looking for you."

"Am I under arrest?" I ask and wipe away a single tear that rolls down my cheek.

"No, not yet, but I will be questioning you and Violet. As soon as Elijah wakes up, we will question him. For now, make sure that you check in with me."

"Yes, I swear to everything holy I'm not going anywhere. Hell, I don't even know when I'm getting sprung out of here. I just woke up. All I know is that it's mid-afternoon."

"Millie, come on," Seth says, tugging on Millie's arm. "She listened to what you had to say, and now we have a funeral to plan. We need to go get an update on Elijah. He needs his parents. Even though I'm not his biological father, I will never turn my back on him. I've raised him since he was born. He may not be mine by blood, but God damn it, he's still my son. And not even you can take that from me."

"Kayla, I'm warning you. Stay away from my family!" Millie shouts.

"Is that a threat, Millie? I don't think Officer Jernigan heard you."

"No dear, it is not a threat," she says, her voice eerily calm, "I was simply telling you to stay away from my son. You've already killed one of them. I don't want to bury the other."

"Millie, I am not even going to try and tell you that it was an accident because you'll believe what you want. Know that I did what I had to do to in order to protect myself and Violet, but I will say he got what he deserved."

"Kayla, you will regret the day you came to live with us!" she was screaming as Seth was pushing her out the door.

"I have always regretted living with you Millie. I wish I had my birth mother, and I never fucking knew you and your stupid ass family."

"Kayla, dear, why don't you rest? I'm going to head to Garret's, and I will check on you later." Patrice leans down and kisses my forehead.

"Dr. Doyle, give me a few minutes, and I'll take you home. Let me give Kayla a kiss and tell her I love her," Garret says, standing up.

"First, Garrett, we're all friends. Please call me Patrice. You stay here with Kayla. She may need you through the night."

"Well, at least let me have Wyatt take you. There is no reason for you to rent a car."

"No Garrett, I'm fine. I'll call a cab and will be back in the morning."

"Patrice, I'd be happy to take you to Garrett's if you want. It is on my way home," Officer Jernigan offers.

"Officer Jernigan, are you flirting with me?"

"Ma'am, I'd be honored if you would allow me to take you home. I know this city like the back of my hand, and I'd hate for you to get lost."

"Officer Jernigan," Patrice begins.

"Please call me Rodney," he interrupts. "I am only Officer Jernigan when I'm at work, and I won't worry about work until tomorrow when I have to write up the reports."

"Okay, Rodney," Patrice says. "If you insist on taking me, then you must know I'm starving. I need to eat, and I'm not one of those salad eating women like you're used to. I like to eat. I'm from Texas, and we eat steak. If you can handle that, then we have a deal. No funny business, you hear me?" She gathers her belongings and tells Rodney she is ready to go.

"After you, Patrice," Rodney says, gesturing to the door.

"You two behave, and don't do anything I wouldn't do, Patrice," I call out.

"Kayla please, if I wanted to *get busy* honey, I would." Patrice replies

"Well, alright then. You have fun, and if you need anything, Patrice, just let me know. The house is stocked though, so you should have everything you need," Garret says.

"Okay Garrett. Thank you so much for everything, and above all, for taking care of Kayla."

"Please, it's my job. I would do anything for her," Garret bends down and kisses me on my temple. "I would move mountains for her Patrice, and one day I will make it official and make her my wife."

"Oh wow," I say. "Garrett, honey, please tell me that is not my proposal because if it is, you suck at being romantic."

"No babe, I promise when it's time to make you mine, I will do it the correct way. It will blow your mind, so don't fret," I whisper in her ear.

"Yeah, I am not even on the page of talking marriage babe."

"Yes Kayla, I know you're not ready for marriage but I hope one day I can change your mind."

"One day, but give me time. "

"Kayla, I will give you as much time as you need. Don't you know I love you, and I'm not ever letting you go again? Now that I have you, it's forever."

Just then the door swings open and a tearful Violet comes running to my bed side.

"You *bitch*, you scared the shit out of me! First, you save my life and then you don't wake up. I'm so proud of you and how you took both those assholes down. Kay, you are the strongest woman I know." VI says all at once.

I look into her eyes and see she is still healing from the beating she took from the fucking Stanton twins.

"VI, I'm so sorry they involved you just to get to me. I'm sorry for everything they did to you." I turn to both VI and Garrett, "This is why I left so none of this would happen. I come home, and what happens? My two best friends are hurt and the only man I ever loved is a wreck because of me," I say and tears start to fall down my face.

Before they can say anything I go on, "Elijah is going to be out for blood since I killed his twin and tried to kill him."

I can't stop the tears now. VI takes one hand and Garrett comes to sit by me on the bed, wrapping me in his arms.

"That scumbag will not hurt you again baby," Garrett says

VI adds, "I'll kill him if he ever comes near you again."

I know they believe what they are saying, but they do not know the real evil he is.

The rest of the night I am restless. I lay in Garrett arms and have nightmares throughout the night.

The next morning Patrice comes in with Officer Jernigan, who asks if he can take my statement of the events and what led up to it.

"I have nothing to hide anymore Officer Jernigan."

"Okay, let's begin," he opens his little notepad and clicks his pen.

"I know these were your adopted brothers, so do you want to tell me why you suspect they were targeting you at *Club Fuchsia* and then going as far as kidnapping your best friend to draw you out?"

"It started when I was a kid. I was physically, emotionally, and mentally abused. I was raped by both of them over and over throughout several years. And then they threatened to get rid of all of those I love. They even said they'd find my birth mother and kill her too. They took VI knowing I would do whatever they wanted to get her back safe and sound. Little did they expect I was ready to fight back for the first time in my life and not submit to their demands."

He motions with his hand for me to go on, so I tell him, "I worked on distracting them long enough to get the gun, and I turned and shot both of them. But I was afraid VI was going to die from the beating and tazing she took."

His questions seemed to go on for hours when in actuality they lasted 45 minutes. By the end I was in tears and told him, "I fear for my life and the lives of those that I love. And once Elijah wakes up, he will be out for blood and will seek revenge for his brother's death. He will think that his brother's death was on my hands. Which I guess it was, but if you want me to say I am sorry Officer Jernigan, I won't say it. "

Officer Jernigan stands from his chair and tells me, "As far as I'm concerned, this was a case of self-defense and no charges will be filed." he turns to Patrice, "I will pick you up after my shift for dinner." He kisses her forehead and turns to walk out of the room, but before he gets out the door he turns to me and says, "Kayla, I will have one of my best men stand guard outside this door until you are released. Then I'll put your home on the patrol unit's route to be passed by every few hours, as well as your friends homes."

The next two days in the hospital drag by before I am finally released to go home. I am getting tired of being poked with freaking needles.

"I told the nurse if she came at me one more time for blood I was going to stab her in the eye with her own damn needle." Of course that got a round of laughter from all who were in here. But I am done, I am ready to go.

"Garrett, please go ask the doctor when I can leave. I am going crazy in here."

"Okay love, I will go ask but you can't be threatening everyone. They are doing their job."

"Shut it Winters. I don't want to hear it. I am ready to go. If it were you here, you would be saying the same thing."

"Possibly love, but just let them do their job without giving them too much grief."

"I can't promise that. I'm sorry I'm being irritable but I know he is here in this hospital and there are only a few floors that are separating me from him. As much as I want to have faith in the Seattle Police Department, they have not always done their jobs before.

"Yes that may be true, but you need to heal and remember Elijah is still in a coma."

"I understand that, but I want to go home and soak in my tub. I want a glass of red wine and I want to just relax. You can't relax in here. There is always something beeping and people constantly checking on you."

"You will be home soon babe and then you and I can soak in the tub together."

"Hey, I never said I wanted you in there with me."

He grabs his heart like I hurt him, and says "Babe, I am sorry but you will no longer be out of site, so suck it buttercup, you are stuck like chuck."

"Ugh, you asshole! You and your brother know I hate being called that!" While rubbing his arm where I gave him a love tap he says "I thought this place was supposed to be a sterile environment? And yes, we know you hate being called that, but seeing how you are basically on bed rest there is nothing you can do about it."

"Oh you just wait, I know how to shut you up...I can just say no."

"Say no to what?" He looks over at me

I smirk, and say, "You are not getting laid for a month of Sundays!"

"Oh Shit, I will be good, I swear."

"Yeah, yeah. Blow it out your ass."

I look at the door, and my nurse is smiling and holding papers in her hand.

"Kayla, I have your discharge papers."

I squeal, and almost jump out of the bed.

"Easy there killer, there are some rules you need to know about."

Damn rules, "Okay, lay them on me."

"First, you are getting out of here because we were told you have someone to take care of you around the clock. Is this true?"

"Yes" I hear in unison from the rat pack—Patrice, Wyatt, Garrett. Rodney shakes his head.

"Well I guess they have spoken for me, so that rule is taken care of. What is next?"

"Second, you are basically on bed rest. No work, no walking around, and no stress."

"Bed rest, really? I feel fine. Why do I need to be on bed rest?"

"Well, I can throw these papers away missy, and you can stay here for the next couple of weeks."

"No, no, no! Bed rest it is," I practically scream at her.

"That's what I thought. Next, if you have any headaches at all, you are to call your doctor. Is that understood?"

"Yes ma'am," I give her a salute.

"I can't stress this enough. No stress Kayla. If you stress, it could cause all kinds of problems for your health. So I just need a signature from you, and then I will take out your IV, and you can be on your way."

"Okay, I will do what you say, I swear, I have been in here long enough and no offense you all are a kick ass staff, but I want my kind sized bed and my seven head shower."

"No offense taken dear. We understand and want you to be able to stay home. That is why the rules of discharge are so important for you to follow."

"We all will make sure she does what she is supposed to do," says Patrice.

"So Kayla, now that I have gone over everything, do you have any questions for me?" the nurse asks.

"No, not that I can think of. I am sure my family here can answer everything for me since they were the ones who were awake when the doctors were talking to me in the beginning. I take that back, I do have one little question?"

"Sure doll, what is it?"

"I'm freaking starving! Can I eat normal food?"

"Ha ha, yes just take it easy. Your throat will be sore for a while because of all the tubes and stuff we had down your throat, but it should be okay within a few days."

"Oh thank god, because I am craving Ivar's."

"That is a good place; just take it easy and you should be fine."

"Thank you so much. I am sorry, but I never even asked your name."

"My name is Kerrigan."

"Oh wow! What a beautiful name. Well I would say that it has been nice knowing you, but to be honest I hope I never see you again. And I mean that with no disrespect."

"Yeah, I know what you mean. None taken. Again, please take care of yourself."

"I will, I promise. Patrice, will you please help me get dressed? And the rest of you, can you wait outside please?"

"Yes Kayla I will," she says, ushering the rest of my dysfunctional family out of the room.

"Thank you for staying Dr. Doyle. I am sure you have other patients."

"Kayla dear, I told you from day one that I would always be here for you. And I have a staff of people who can work for me at any time."

"I just want you to know that it means the world that you are here. You know that I have longed for my birth mother, and well, you are the closest thing I have to a mother."

"Oh Kayla honey, you just made my day because I think of you like a daughter as well."

I get up and hug her neck and I see a tear roll down her cheek.

"Hey Patrice, can I ask you something?"

"Sure, you know you can ask me anything."

"The other day when Millie was in here, she said we all have secretes. What did she mean when she said that?

"Oh, it was nothing worth talking about. One day I will tell you all about me, but let's get you better first?"

"Okay, but you know I will not forget about this."

"Yes Kayla, I know this all too well. I promise one day, when I know there will be no interruptions, I will tell you but not right now. Let's get you dressed so that you can go home and relax. You may as well accept it because that's all you will be doing."

"Yeah, please don't remind me. Before I get too relaxed, I need to call and check in with my job. Hell, I don't even know if I still have a job. I hope so because my medical bills are going to be off the charts."

"Your work will be there in a couple of weeks dear. You are going to do what the doctor said. You are going to relax and nothing else, do you understand me?"

"Geez, I got it drill sergeant," I smile at her, grab my bags of stuff, and open the door. When I look down, I see my chariot—the wheelchair they make you ride in when being discharged.

I look over at Garrett, and he smiles at me before saying, "Get in my lady, and I will be your escort for the ride down."

Something about that man gives me goose bumps in my lady parts. Damn I can't wait to get home so I can do some naughty things to him.

CHAPTER TWO

Finally Home

"Don't be pushed by your problems. Be led by your dreams."

~Ralph Waldo Emerson

I'm finally going home. Garrett is driving me, and I am gazing out the window wondering what Elijah is going to try to do next. I'm startled when I feel a hand squeeze mine as a tear falls from my eye.

"Kayla? Baby, please don't cry. I can handle anyone else crying, but you I can't. Let's wipe those tears and get you safely inside your house." Garrett says, kissing the back of my hand as he pulls into my driveway.

"If only you knew the fear I keep bottled within. I keep it from you and the others in order to protect you. Babe, if you only knew the pure hell they put me through. You know everything I went through because I have shared everything with you, but you can't experience the feelings. Knowing is not the same as reliving every minute of every day of torture. If you could experience those feelings—my feelings, then you might understand how afraid I am."

I'm scared shitless for me and for my little family. No, we aren't a blood family, but these misfits are the only family I have, and I'll be damned if I let some trifling, Twatwaffle destroy what little bit of happiness I have.

A few seconds later, he is coming around the truck and lifting me out. Instead of placing me on the ground, he carries me into my home and manages to disarm both security systems I have in place. At last, he sets me down on the sofa and asks me what I would like for dinner.

I tell him Chinese, and he has it delivered, but while we are waiting the 50 minutes for delivery, he runs a hot bath for me to soak in and wash away the grime from the hospital stay and the events that led up to it. While I'm soaking, I have music playing softly in the background, and I'm trying my best to keep my mind off of anything to do with Elijah and what he might do if he gets his hands on me again. The worst thing I'm trying to avoid is what I am going to have to do to keep my loved ones safe. When I come out of the bathroom wrapped in a pink towel and my hair pulled up and wrapped in another pink towel. I dry off and soon I'm in my comfortable clothes; an over-sized shirt, some boxer briefs, and yoga pants.

I go downstairs to find Garrett has the table set. The food is served and there are even candles lit in the center of the table. His chair is next to mine so we can have a romantic dinner, and the sweetest song is playing in the background. I could not even tell you what song it was because it was just an instrumental version.

Garrett walks over and takes my hand, kissing my cheek and then my lips. He tells me I look beautiful. I watch as he walks to the table, pulling me behind him.

He pulls out my chair and allows me to sit before taking a seat himself. A true gentleman. How lucky am I?

We make small talk as we eat, and every once in a while he'll feed me a bite of his food.

"Babe, why are you not eating?" he asks as he moves closer to me and kisses me on the cheek.

"I'm sorry. It's hard to eat when I know either Millie or Elijah will try and do something. I know you think I'm crazy, but the look in her eyes when she found out that Edwin died was pure hatred. I always knew she was not my biggest supporter, and I think her telling me all the shit she did that day was just to make her look good. I know there will be major problems. She is not going to let this go. According to her, I killed her son. Yes, I guess you could say that I did, but I was tired of him hurting me and the people close to me. I will never forgive myself for them hurting VI, and I could kick her ass for going there in the first place. Is she fucking insane?"

"Okay, let's deal with one thing at a time. First of all, you are safe. You are here at home, and there is safety in numbers. Second, VI is a grown woman, and you know as well as I do that there is no stopping her once she has her mind made up. And third, I would have done the same thing as her. She beat me to it. So if she is insane, I will be right there rocking in my straight jacket beside her. Come on babe...that was supposed to be a joke. You know, *ha-ha, funny*."

"I just don't see the humor in all of this. Wyatt was hurt, VI was almost raped, and you are over here cracking fucking jokes. It is not comedy hour at the

Apollo Garrett. This is real fucking life. They are not sitting back and laying low. I will swear on my life that Millie is planning something. I can feel it."

"Okay, so say you're right babe. What are you going to do about it?"

"I won't tell you my plans Garrett because I don't want Officer Jernigan to get you with accessory to any of my possible crimes.

"I will not let you go half-cocked to deal with the crazies on your own. So I expect you to be honest with me. Kayla, I love you and I want to protect you, but I can't do that if you won't let me in on your plans. I am not some weak man, so please don't treat me as one. I know you are thinking, I can see the wheels turning in your beautiful head, but I know I am not going to get any answers right now but I am telling you I will not drop this."

"Okay. Garrett let's clean up and then watch a movie."

After we cleared our plates, we laid on the sofa together. I lay in his arms and finally feel myself begin to relax. I lift my head off of Garrett's chest and kiss him softly, slowly, and seductively.

Garrett kisses me back with the same passion I am giving him, and he brings his arms around my body a little tighter. I lean up and grasp his face, and as I deepen the kiss, I am wanting more.

I want to feel him inside of me. No, I *need* to feel him inside of me. I whisper, "Make love to me."

He smiles and says "Baby, you don't know how long I've waited for you to say those words to me. I thought I lost you, and when I got you back in the hospital, the only thing I wanted was for you to wake up so I can make sweet, passionate love to the only woman I have ever loved and will ever love."

I am now sitting up and I am undressing him when he tells me to take it slow.

I roll us over, and he nudges my legs open and lays between them. He kisses my lips and moves to nibble along my jaw. Following the contours, he finds my earlobe and sucks gently. Never remaining in one place too long, he trails kisses down my neck and across my throat until he reaches my T-shirt.

He rips the shirt over my head and finds I'm not wearing a bra. His lips roam across my collarbone and then to my taut nipple. He plays with it a split second before taking it into his mouth. He sucks and flicks it with his tongue.

Garrett tortures me with his mouth while his thumb and forefinger are on the other nipple.

I am craving more and I have a tingling in my core. Garrett's hands glide down my body, pulls off my yoga pants and boxers as his lips trail down my body, stopping to kiss in between my hipbones.

All of a sudden his head dips between my legs and he starts licking and sucking on my swollen clit. I feel one, then two fingers slowly slip inside of me massaging the front wall of my pussy. It drives me insane. I grab his hair and pull him in even more, wrapping my legs around his shoulders. As I begin to climax I call out his names, and he doesn't stop until I cum.

I glance down at him and he's looking up at me, licking his lips, "You're the best dessert I could ever fucking have."

He then crawls back up my body and plunges his tongue into my mouth. I can taste my juices on his tongue and it excites me. I feel the head of his cock at the entrance of my core, and then he enters me slowly. I moan loudly, making him stop for a second. I want to enjoy this moment, I pull him closer so that he is now all the way inside me. We have a rhythm all our own, and I see fireworks in my head. This man knows how to make my body scream and quiver. We slow dance with each other, a dance only unique to us.

"God I have missed this," I whisper.

He says "You have no idea. Your body was made for me. We fit perfectly together."

We take it slow and make love to each other before we both collapse. Slow kisses from him send chills all over my body.

Garrett is on the side of me and pulls me into his arms, kissing my neck. Then he turns my head so my ear is right next to his mouth and he whispers "You're safe with me."

I turn my head with sleepy eyes, give him a kiss, and all I can say is I love you. I hear him say I love you too, and then I must drift to sleep—the first restful sleep I've gotten since I've woken up. He is like a security blanket that I can wrap my soul in.

The next day I wake up in my bed, wrapped in Garrett's arms. He must've carried me up to bed at some point during the night. I don't even remember falling asleep. But after a night of love making, and just getting out of the hospital I was exhausted.

I know today is Edwin's funeral, and if I'm not there to see the evil monster go into the ground, never to come out of it again, then I will never truly have closure. I have to see it to believe it.

I know that I am not welcome, but I have to start to come up with a plan. When I try getting out of the bed Garrett wraps his arms tight around me and asks, "Where are you going baby?"

I give him a quick kiss and tell him I need to take a quick shower but today is the funeral and I have to be there.

Garrett jumps to his feet and screams "Are you fucking kidding me? You are not going to that funeral."

I look him dead in the eyes and tell him if I don't go I will never have closure.

"Babe, you know you are not welcome there."

I give him a small smile and tell him I have a plan and that I need him to be there by my side.

He walks over to me, kisses me quickly and says "I'm not leaving your side, no matter what your crazy ass wants to do. I will be right there with you." He takes my hand as we go into the shower and emerge quickly, dressing in black. I am wearing a pair of black skinny jeans, a charcoal sweater, and thigh-high boots. I grab a black jacket and get dressed to look the part of a person in mourning—not that I'm in mourning, but I don't want to stand out. I look the part of a grieving family member. I throw some water-proof mascara on my eyes and some simple pink gloss on my lips.

Before long we head to Lakeview Memorial Cemetery in Seattle. Garrett and I are keeping a safe distance and bringing flowers to an unknown grave. We act as though we are just there to pay our respects to that person. I look at the graves of so many people along the way. There are some celebrities buried here such as Martial-arts film star Bruce Lee and his son, Brandon Lee.

So not to draw attention to ourselves, we watch the services and I am shocked to see Jason Woodrow there. I'm even more shocked to witness a confrontation and words are exchanged between him and Seth. I whisper to Garrett, "Look, Raegan's dad is here." I can tell this is going to be good.

I can hear Jason's raised voice saying, "If I would've raised those boys, my son would still be alive, but no, you had to raise them and let one get killed and the other be put in a medically induced coma. It's because you can't control them and their actions," then goes on to say "Millie never told me I was a father. I would have taken care of them had I known."

Seth voice raises and tells him "Those are my sons! Get the fuck off of my son's grave, or I will have you forcibly removed. I have raised him since birth." That's when Jason swings a right hook at Seth, who takes a step back and jabs Jason in the nose with an uppercut, knocking him to the ground.

After getting on top of Jason, Seth starts to pound him. There is blood on both of them, torn shirts and bruised egos.

Jason is able to roll them over and take control of the fight, beating Seth. Jason punches him in the ribs and then goes to Seth's face which is bloody. Both men are winded.

Both men are saying *that was my son*. Eventually, some of the onlookers break up the fight that is sure to be on the ten o'clock news. With all the media surrounding this funeral, I'm sure they captured everything on camera. Millie is screaming at both of them, causing more of a problem.

Soon though, everyone leaves the cemetery and it is quiet. I am in tears. I am so angry and upset that I drag Garrett to the grave. I fall to my knees and start pounding my fist into the fresh dirt. I am taking all my anger out on the ground. Dirt is flying everywhere. I spit on the dirt, only to hit it again with my fist. I start cussing out Edwin for everything he's done to me, calling him a fucking bastard and I'm screaming how much I hated him. "You fucking prick, I hate you! I am glad you are dead! I hope you are enjoying Hell!"

I then feel Garrett's arms wrap around me and he tells me, "Baby let's go!"

I say hell no, and I stand up, grab him, and kiss him with everything I have. I tell him I need him—here and now, hard and rough.

He looks at me dumbfounded, but he grabs and kisses me and says, "If you need me baby, you got me."

I try to unbutton his jeans. But he stops my hands.

"No, not here. We are not going to have sex on this grave Kayla. I know that you are hurt and you have every right to be, but you are not going to sink to his level."

"Garrett, please take away all the pain." I slap my fist onto his chest.

"Kayla you can hit me all you want if that will make you fill better. I will be your punching bag."

I try again to get into his pants. He throws me over his shoulder. I'm kicking and screaming at him to put me down.

"I will not put you down, I am going to take you home, where you can calm down."

"Why are you such an asshole?" I scream.

We get to the truck and he literally throws me in the truck and slams the door. I am stunned because I have never seen him like this.

"Kayla, normally I don't say much, I accept that you have issues with them, but to try to have sex on a dead man's grave? You need to get yourself together!"

"Don't you dare tell me I need to get myself together, you have no fucking clue how he hurt me!"

"Kayla, you are acting like a child. Yes he hurt you, but the man is dead. You watched him get put into the damn ground. Do you really think it's okay to have sex there?"

"I just wanted him to know that he has no power over me any longer." "Do you know how to take your power back Kayla?" "No, I don't Garrett." I say crying. "You have faith in yourself. You hold the power, not them. Take your power back. Show the world that you are better because of your past. Don't be a statistic."

I never thought Edwin's death would make me feel like this. I am so pissed at him. I have wanted him dead for years, but I am also torn. He was always the lesser of the two evils. When his brother was harsh and cold, he was caring and warm. I know it sounds crazy to think like that of someone who hurt you, but I always thought Elijah was the leader and Edwin just followed. He did what he was told to do.

Though I am still in tears, I can't believe I was so enraged at the gravesite that I did that to Garrett, but the entire way home he tells me not to worry about it. He's there for whatever I need, whenever I need it.

Today, I needed him more than I need anything else. He took every hit I gave him today.

CHAPTER THREE

A Night Out

"If things seem under control, you are just not going fast enough."

~Mario Andretti

While we are driving, I decide I do not want to go home so I tell Garrett to take me to the club. I am tired of sitting at home and it has been less than twenty four hours since I was released from the hospital. After telling Garrett, I call VI and tell her and Wyatt need to meet us there.

VI says "Great! They have an awesome band playing called Jaded. Besides, we can all use the night out and a good time after everything that's happened"

I hang up with VI, and Garrett turns the beast in the direction of the club. He grabs my hand and says, "Babe, are you sure you want to go back to the club?"

"Yes, I'm sure. I know what happened last time we were there, but I need to get out of the house before I lose my damn mind."

"Okay babe, I was just making sure. I know you hate sitting around and not doing anything but you need to rest."

"Yeah, yeah. I know I do but give me tonight please. Let me just enjoy a night out, and I swear on my pink Coach purse I will lay low tomorrow."

"Wow! Swearing on a pink Coach purse. You must mean business because that's like a Bible for you."

"Why yes dear it is. That is why I swore on it instead of the Bible. If I swear on a Bible, I might go to hell, but if I swear on my purse, you know I mean business."

"Touche' babe, touché."

It doesn't take us long to get to the club. When we pull in, I see Wyatt's crotch rocket parked right up front and VI's car around the side. That lets me know they are here already. Before Garrett can even shut off my SUV, I am out and headed for the door.

Once outside the door, we find VI and Wyatt waiting for us at the V.I.P. entrance.

We make our way inside and I'm surprised. The band is kick ass.

Garrett and I are on the dance floor bumping and grinding to the music. He's covering me in kisses, not giving a fuck who sees. Quite frankly, I don't either. I look around and suddenly see the bitch Reagan walk up. Garrett must see it too because he takes my hand and leads me back to the table where VI and Wyatt are waiting with our drinks. Unfortunately, she follows us.

I sit on Garrett's lap, and Reagan becomes enraged. She is ranting that I stole her man, and she has come to claim what is hers.

I get up in her face and tell her if she doesn't get out of my face I'm going to knock her for a fucking loop. I'm so not in the mood to play her games. I watch her turn around, thinking she was leaving, however the bitch grabs a drink from the table and has the balls to throw it into my face. Before I can react, VI snaps and spins out of control.

She screams, "I whooped your skanky ass in school, and I will do it again. Reagan didn't you get the memo, you are old news. He doesn't want you. He has moved on to greener pastures. So bye Felicia!"

She grabs Reagan by the hair and slams her head onto the table. She then pushes her onto the ground, straddles her waist, and pounds on her face. Reagan tries to block the blows, and VI moves to her ribs. VI hits her over and over. Finally VI gets up, grabs Reagan by the hair, and pulls her to her feet, dragging her out of the club. There is a crowd gathering and VI doesn't want witnesses.

I follow to make sure she doesn't completely lose all self-control. When I walk into the night air, I see her throw Reagan into her car. Yes, the little red car I saw that I thought was one of the bastards had traded their truck for. The one I saw when I was headed to the boat house to save VI.

Of course this enrages me even more, but I hear VI say, "If you ever come near Kayla or Garrett again, I swear to God I will make your life a living hell. After what you allowed to be done to me, you're lucky I don't shoot you here and now on the spot!"

"Garrett, will be my man again, you wait. He will grow tired of the used up wanna-be."

VI reaches into her purse and pulls out a Taser. Hell, I didn't know she even had one. Before I can react, VI is touching Reagan with it. She starts burning the bitch's chest screaming, "How the fuck do you like it you cunt? You stood there and watched them do this to me now it's your turn to live with scars. How does it feel bitch?" I have never seen VI like this.

VI then turns and walks away. She spots me at the corner of the building and makes her way toward me. She breaks down and cries, "That bitch saw what they did to me and did nothing to stop them."

"Kayla, all she was after was getting Garrett away from you. She didn't care what they did to me or you."

"She's lucky I don't shoot her here on the spot."

I hold her in my arms and tell her, "She will get hers when the time is right, but right now is not the time. We need to pull ourselves together."

I give her a moment to compose herself. I see the fucking trick and I walk over to the car. I spit in the bitch's face and pull her by the hair to look at me. When I see her face, I punch her five times and tell her if she ever lays a finger on my best friend again or let anything happen to her or even attempt to come near my man, she hasn't seen who the real threat is yet.

"I'm the bitch not to be fucked with!" I slam her head on the steering wheel, knocking her out. I turn around and walk back to VI.

I am thankful that no one is in the parking lot to see what has happened. I know where the cameras are and I hope that none of them are situated to spot that bitch's car or record what has been done, but if so, we will deal with it when the time comes.

"Come on gutterslut, let's go get our men and work off some steam on the dance floor. I need a damn drink."

She looks down at her hands and sees the blood, and I pull her into the club and make a beeline to the employee lounge and immediately lock the door.

"Come on babe, let's get you cleaned up."

She looks up at me and wipes her face, and for the first time I actually see her tear soaked face. Her mascara is running down her face. And I see what looks like a fat lip. I grab the first aid kit and start to clean her up. She is trembling, and crying.

"Kay, I am so sorry. It's always drama with her and I was fed up. I could not take it anymore."

"Shhhhh, you have nothing to be sorry for. She had it coming. And when did you get a damn Taser? I knew about your gun because, well hell, I have shot that, but a Taser too?"

"Kayla, I bought it after my last run in with her. I knew that I'd see her ass again and I wanted to make sure she would feel the same pain I felt. I am not playing anymore. She better hope and pray that I don't see her in a dark place around town, because I swear to everything holy, I will kill her."

"Geez, Vi, tell me how you really feel."

"Anyway, enough about her, I don't want to hear her name for the remainder of the night. Let's go find those Winter men. I'm sure they are freaking the fuck out."

"We have been gone for a while now. So, speaking of the Winter men, are you and Wyatt like together, you know, have you guys made it Facebook official yet? Because you know unless it's online you are not official."

"No gutterslut, we have not given it a label or title. We're having fun, and he is sooooo much fun!"

"Okay, no labels, I got you. Does he know you're in love with him?"

"Wait! Who said anything about love?" VI asks.

"You didn't have to say it VI. I know you. You're my sister from another mister. You can try hiding it from Wyatt, but you can't hide it from me no matter how hard you try.

"Kay, yes, I love him, but I am not going to be the first to say those words. I don't have to worry about him saying that because Ariel broke his heart, and he has made it clear that there will never be anything serious."

"I don't know about that. I see the way he looks at you. I saw the look on his face when you were in trouble. He loves you too. Wyatt may not be ready to admit it, but he loves your ass despite your reluctance to admit it to the world. Okay, I see the look you are giving me. Enough with the heavy talk. Let's go dance and have fun, but know a good man like him won't remain single forever."

"Kayla, I love you to the moon and back, but if you open your big mouth to Wyatt, I swear I will sneak in your house and destroy all your shoes, and then pour bleach on everything you own that is pink."

VI is laughing so hard, I think she may fall down. I hold my hands up to surrender. When my shoes and signature color are threatened, I know when to surrender despite VI's joking.

"That is what I thought you ass. I mean it—keep your trap shut."

I raise my hands and do the scouts honor, and she hits my shoulder and we both start laughing.

"Damn. Did you guys fall in the bathroom or something? Is everything okay? After Reagan showing up here, I want to make sure you are fine." A strong, familiar voice whispers in my ear. I turn around and see Garrett's sexy face.

"I am fine. She does not worry me. It was only girl talk, and then someone in there needed a tampon, so I went out to the beast and got her one.

I see VI look at me and I know she will have my back. Though I am not worried, I don't think he would care that his ex is sitting in the parking lot with a broken nose and now has some wicked scars.

After we get back in the club, VI takes Wyatt by the hand and drags him into the VIP lounge. The next thing we hear are her screams. Flashbacks of the first night I was here came into mind, how I had watched Wyatt and VI. Suddenly, I was turned on. I grabbed Garrett and lead him into Wyatt's office.

"Babe, where are we going? I thought we were going to the dance floor."

"No. I have other plans for us at this moment." I rub his cock through his jeans as I drag him into the office. Slamming the door behind us, I push him against it and lock the knob.

"Babe, normally I would not complain, but we are in a public place."

"Shut it Winters, a girl has needs. And right now I need you. I have his pants undone and I am on my knees, within a second I have his dick in my mouth. I take long slow licks and then I suck on the mushroomed head. I cup his balls and use my other hand while using my mouth on his dick. My assault on him makes him weak in the knees, and I can feel his knees shaking. I peer up at him through my lashes and notice that his eyes are rolling in the back of his head. I go for the gusto and I take him all the way into the back of my throat and it doesn't take long. I can feel that he is close. I sneak my finger into his ass and that is all it takes. I now taste his thick cum. His balls tighten, and I am milking him. I take every last drop and then swallow it all. I clean him up with my tongue and kiss the head.

I start to stand up and the next thing I know I am turned around and my face is pushed up against the wall. My jeans are being pushed down around my ankles. He is reaching his hand under my shirt and has my nipple in his hands. Within seconds he is inside me, thrusting and making me scream out his name. We have never had sex like this and I fucking love it. I tell him to fuck me harder and I feel a slap on my ass before his hands wrap around my throat. He whispers, "Your pussy is like a fucking drug. One taste and you're fucking addicted."

I push my ass into him and he takes his other hand and has found my clit. He is fucking me from behind and has a hold of my clit with his thumb and I am seeing stars.

"Babe, tell me whose pussy this is."

"It's yours!" I scream.

"Are you sure? I don't know, maybe I should stop."

"Don't you fucking dare" I scream "This is your pussy, baby. Now fuck me harder!"

He pumps a couple more times and we come together. We are both breathing heavy but he pulls my face towards him and gives me the most passionate kiss I have ever had.

"Kayla honey, what are you doing to me? I am not someone who has sex in public places, but today we almost had sex on the grave of a dead man and now my brother's office. I swear I am not complaining so don't take it that way, but are you sure you are okay?"

I stand there for a minute just looking at him, I shake my head and tell him I am fine. "Don't worry about me babe. I promise if something is bothering me I will let you know."

"But I do worry. I know that you still have your demons you are working through, but I am here. Please don't leave me out of the loop. I will listen and I won't judge."

"I know that babe, but I am fine. Now let's go get a drink because I am suddenly thirsty. You wouldn't happen to know why, would you?" I ask, laughing and pull my jeans up and adjust my bra so that I am fully covered.

The steady beat of the music is hypnotic and I catch myself swaying to the beat. Garrett grabs my hand and leads me on the dance floor. He is holding me close and we are slow dancing to Ed Sheeran's *Thinking Out Loud*. Garrett is singing the words to me and it melts my heart. I whisper, "I love you Garrett."

He places my hand on his heart and says "Babe, you have my heart and I love you too. "

I kiss him softly on the dance floor while we are swaying back and forth. There is a room full of people around us, but I don't see anyone, just him. It is like time stands still during this song.

The next thing I know the song is over and I am being led over to the bar.

"Hey Buttercup, that was some hot moves out there on the dance floor." Wyatt says playfully.

"Hey don't be jealous Wyatt. I know how to make my man happy."

"Oh believe me. Vi makes me very happy." Wyatt says.

"Yeah the whole club knows how happy she makes you." I look over to VI and I could see she doesn't care that the whole club heard her have sex.

She looks over at me and says, "Sorry about that, but I was horny and wanted to get laid. It is not my fault that I am a vocal person."

"Let's go. I'm beat. It has been a long day and I am ready for my bed."

"Vi, are you coming home with me or you going to Kayla's?" Wyatt asks.

"Everyone can stay at my house. I have plenty of room."

CHAPTER FOUR

The Past Always Comes Back

"My life is perfect, even when it is not."

~Ellen Degeneres

Kayla and VI are both passed out in the beast and my baby looks like an angel. I see her smile in her sleep and I hope that she is finally having good dreams.

Once we were back at Kayla's, Wyatt and I carry the girls inside and put them to bed. I take a quick shower and brush my teeth then I go down to the kitchen for a snack while Kayla sleeps. I am walking down the hallway when angry voices greet me and fill every room of the house. Who the fuck is here? I peer around the corner, and I see Patrice talking to Seth.

"Patrice, I know damn well you remember our night in college," Seth states.

"You mean the night you raped me? I was a virgin you motherfucker. I know you slipped something in my drink because I only had one drink and there was no way I was willing."

"Our night together was magical. I didn't have to rape you, you were more than willing. Besides, you know as well as I do that Kayla is your daughter as much as she is mine." He states.

"If you knew she was your daughter, how could you let what happened to her happen, and then treat her like nothing?" Patrice says crying.

"I didn't know then, but I know now. I knew the moment I saw you standing by her bedside in the hospital. I knew you looked familiar. I would remember you anywhere."

"That doesn't mean she's my daughter, but I do care for her. I don't know what happened to my daughter. I gave her up at the hospital. I never even held her. The only thing I remember from giving birth is how perfect her little cry was. They rushed her out of the room, and I cried myself to sleep that night. I could hear her crying all night long. So I left the next morning before staff change."

"You are in fucking denial woman. That girl is ours."

"Seth, I want you to keep your god damned mouth shut. Your family has hurt her enough, and she does not need any more fucking stress. If you so much as look in her fucking direction, I swear on everything I hold dear, I will kill you. And you can take that to the damn bank" Patrice screams.

I can't believe what I am hearing, and I know it will kill Kayla to hear this. I don't know what to do. I can't tell her, and it takes everything I have not to go into that room and beat the fuck out of Seth for what he did to Patrice, and most of all, what he let be done to Kayla. At one point I really respected Seth. He had promise as a kick ass senator, and most likely would have made for a damn good president. But now that I know him, I am glad that he has taken a back seat in politics.

I quietly head back to our bedroom, crawl into bed, and hold Kayla close. I can't help but wonder how in the hell she'll survive this. She will be crushed to know Seth is her father, though I know she will be happy to hear she has a mother. But she can't know this. With a heavy heart I sigh and try to sleep. I toss and turn and listen for Kayla's steady breathing. That is somewhat calming but I know her life is about to change, I just have to figure out how to tell her.

I fell in love with her back in St. James church when she was teaching me how to read. Even when I was going to be married to the gold digging whore, I was picturing Kayla walking down the aisle. That was the last thing I thought of before falling into a restless sleep.

The next morning we wake to the smells of coffee and pancakes. When we get downstairs, we find the news declaring Seth has officially pulled out of the presidential race. The rumor is he pulled out because of the scandal regarding his family.

"About damn time," Wyatt declares as he walks around and kisses the top of Kayla's head. He walks to VI and wraps his arm around her waist and pulls her to his side.

"I would kiss you, but I have a major case of morning breath." VI tells Wyatt.

"Awe, babe you know I don't mind your breath anytime."

"No! That's gross! Don't come near me." VI mumbles as she is covering her mouth with her hand. "Sorry you are just S.O.L. There will be no kissing until I have coffee and get the funk out of my mouth. So just calm your jets there big boy."

"Damn! No love this morning. You suck babe."

"We all know I suck, and that I swallow too, but until I have coffee and brush my teeth, there will be no kissing, so suck it up buttercup."

"Awe, aren't you guys so freaking cute. Wyatt dear, when are you going to make an honest woman of VI?

"Kayla geez, you made me spit out my coffee. You ass," VI says.

"I thought you said you swallow? I guess you spit as well," I go over and give her a big hug, "it's okay if you spit." I hit her on her arm and tell her I love her fucking face.

Patrice comes out of the guest room looking like she saw a ghost. She won't look at me—in fact, she says her goodbye using the excuse she's going back to Garrett's place to get ready for a date with Rodney.

I tell her bye and ask her if everything is okay.

"Yeah, everything is fine. Don't worry," she says rushing to the door.

When she opens the door, Rodney is standing there, fist raised to knock on the door. He doesn't waste any time and asks Garrett to go to the station to answer a few questions about Seth's attack.

"Babe, do you want me to go with you?"

"No. Stay here and rest. I am sure it won't take long." He says and kisses me on the forehead.

"Okay, I love you."

"I love you too babe," he kisses me again—this time, softly on the lips.

I watch him walk out the door. I turn and run into Patrice.

"I am so sorry, Patrice. I did not mean to run into you."

"Kayla, it is okay, but I really have to go."

Next thing I know, the door is being slammed behind her.

"VI, do you know what is going on with Patrice?"

"No, I was just about to ask you the same thing."

"Has something happened back in Texas with her practice or something? I swear she was fine yesterday. I will get to the bottom of this, but first, I am going to go and get dressed and then go to the police station. I want to be there with Garrett because this is my fault after-all."

"Kayla, it isn't your fault. Garrett is a grown man who was trying to find his woman." Wyatt says.

"You were there too, weren't you Wyatt?"

"Yes buttercup, I was there. I was the one who gave him the black eye."

"So there is no way he can get into trouble over this, right?"

"Well, I can't answer that because we did go over to his house. We did kind of interrupt Seth's sexual encounter, and then he proceeded to get a beating that he had coming."

"You mean you guys walked in while he was having sex with Millie?"

"Oh no, Millie walked us back to the pool house, and he had some young intern bent over the pool table." Wyatt said.

"Oh my god, are you freaking serious? Millie was there when he was having sex with someone else? That family is dysfunctional."

"Well, they surely put the FUN in dysfunctional." VI piped in.

"You are so right VI. Now I have to go and get dressed so I can go check on Garrett."

"Okay. Love your face."

"Love yours too, gutterslut." I yell from the hallway.

I walk into my big, over-stuffed closet and pick out a pair of black leggings and a hot pink long sweater. Before walking out, I grab a grey and pink scarf and my black faux suede and thigh high boots. I don't even bother taking a shower. I spray on some Wings perfume and get dressed.

I throw my hair up in a loose bun and grab my purse and head out to the beast. Jumping inside, I pull out and make my way to the police station. In the parking lot, I throw the beast into park and head into the building through the double glass doors. I walk in like I've been there a million times before.

CHAPTER FIVE
Dealing with the Truth

"When you reach the end of your rope, tie a knot and hang on."

~Franklin D. Roosevelt

When I get down to the station, Rodney takes me into an interrogation room and starts asking me questions.

"Garrett, how long have you had a grudge against Seth?"

"I would not say it was a grudge. I just don't like the man." I tell him.

"Have you ever passed by his house with the intent to hurt him?"

"Hell no. I run a successful publishing company. I don't have time for plotting to hurt some low life. And yes I know that comment makes me look guilty but to be honest, it was about time he felt some of the pain Kayla has felt for years."

"Son, I won't say he didn't, but you and your brother really put a beating on him."

"Yes, I know this, and if we have to, we will do what it takes to make it right, but I had to find my love. I have seen the way you are toward Patrice. Can you tell me that you would not have done the same thing if you knew she was hurt?"

"Off the record, you are right but I still have to ask these questions."

"I know what is next. I have nothing to hide Officer Jernigan."

"I have just one last question Garrett, and this one is the most important of all questions. How long have you known Kayla was his daughter and Patrice was her mother?"

When that question was asked, we heard glass shattering and ran to see what was going on out there.

I see Kayla, and she has tears running down her beautiful face. She has a cut on her hand and it is bleeding badly.

One cop is cleaning up the broken glass and another is bandaging her hand.

All she says to me is, "How could you? You are supposed to love me."

She starts beating on my chest and screaming profanities. Kayla is crying and she never cries.

It takes two cops to pull her off me. Then one tells me to head home—the interview is over.

I tell the officer that the only home I am going to is Kayla's because I have to fix things.

I will not lose her over some half ass conversation I overheard. There is no fucking way in hell I will allow this to break us.

We have been through way too much for something like this to damage our relationship, so I go and wait by the beast for her to come out.

***

I sit in one of the interrogation rooms while a cop, who moonlights as an EMT, bandages up my hand. For one split second I wondered what it would have been like just to end it right then and there. I could have with the shattered glass. I could have bent down and picked up a piece and ended it all. But that is the coward's way out and I am not a fucking coward.

After they are done bandaging me up, I grab my purse and walk out the doors. I look out to my beast, and I see him standing there. I hold out my hand telling him to shut his mouth but I know I have unfinished business. If he kept something like this from me, then what future do we have?

"Garrett, I am mad at you. Why in the hell did you think it was okay to keep something like this from me?"

"Babe, please let me explain, I swear I only learned about this last night when we came home from the club. You had fallen asleep, and I carried you up too bed. I grabbed a quick shower, headed down stairs, and I overheard Patrice and Seth screaming at each other."

"Why didn't you wake me up? Or better yet you could have told me this morning. But oh no, you kept this from me. How can I ever trust you?"

"Honey please, I wanted to make sure before I said anything. I know how you wanted to find your birth mother. And I would have never wanted to give you false hope. If I would have said anything I would not have had any proof."

"Garrett, you kept something huge from me."

"But you've kept things from me. Such as your rape?"

"That is different. You all know why I did that. I was trying to protect you all."

"Yes dear, I get that, but you did keep that from me. I know it's not the same, but I wanted to make sure of the facts, and not come at you with half ass answers."

"I guess I see where you would want to wait, but how can I trust you? How can we have a future if you are going to keep things from me?"

"Kayla baby, I love you more than life itself. I would never intentionally keep things from you. If it makes you feel any better, I wanted to go downstairs and beat the shit out of Seth. Babe, all I am going to say is listen to Patrice, hear her side before you just write her off. Please listen to her."

"What are you not telling me?"

"Kayla, let's go home and you talk to her. She will tell you what you need to know. All I ask is that you fully listen, not just with your ears but listen with your heart. It has never guided you in the wrong direction."

"Okay, get in and let's go, but I am still pissed at you and you have some major ass kissing to do."

"Honey, if you forgive me I would gladly kiss your ass every minute of every day. Look baby I know you are mad at me, and I know you feel I betrayed you, but I love you and I know we can get past this if we try."

"Just get in the beast Garrett."

Before he can talk or say a word, I hold up my hand and say, "Look, I love you, and I don't want to lose you, but I am not ready to talk right now."

When we pull up at my house, Patrice's car is there along with Wyatt and VI's.

Garrett and I walk in the house, and they see the look on my face. I can tell they know something happened.

"Patrice and Kayla need to go talk alone, and I stress the alone part."

Patrice, looks over at me, and I can see she knows that I know.

"Kayla come on. I know that you have questions, and I will do what I can to answer them for you."

CHAPTER SIX

Old Skeletons

"Forgiveness means letting go of the past."

~Gerald Jampolsky

"Patrice, when were you going to tell me?" I demand to know as soon as we got into my office. I did not even give Patrice a chance to close the door.

"Kayla sweetie, calm down. This is not something we know for sure. We have to do a DNA test."

"And don't Kayla sweetie me. Fuck! A DNA test? Did you know this whole time? All this time Patrice? You have been my confidant. I trusted you. I am so angry I don't even have the words at how upset I am. Did you suspect it all this time? What about all the times I asked about my birth mother? How many times have I told you I wanted to find her and yet you said nothing? You said not one fucking word. Why now?"

"Kayla calm down so we can talk about this as adults."

"Fuck that! Where were you when I was being raped and tortured? How can you even stand here and be so damned calm? This not only affects my life but yours as well. Why not come find me? How can you say you love me, when you lied to my face every day for years?"

"Kayla I am not going to say it again. Calm down and allow me to explain things to you."

"Don't pull that mother tone with me. You have no right to tell me to calm down. I won't calm down until there is a fucking DNA test and I know if you betrayed me or not."

"Kayla, damn it, listen to me! I never betrayed you. I never had proof. If you want a DNA test, I'll have Rodney have one ran. Yes, you have the right to be mad and upset with me but please do not speak to me like I don't care about you."

"I will talk to you any damn way I want right now." Suddenly I collapse into my desk chair in tears and I can't pull myself together. Patrice runs to my side but I yell at her, "Don't you dare touch me. I need to be alone to think. Please get out."

"Okay Kayla, I will leave right now, but I am not leaving the house. We will continue this conversation later, after we both have time to think. I am truly sorry. And I hope that you can forgive me."

"I have one question for you Patrice."

"Okay, I will answer anything you ask." Patrice says as she is wiping a tear from her face.

"Did you love him?"

"Kayla, I was in college, and I went to a party. I had one drink, just one. I set my drink down for literally two minutes, and when I came back into the room, I drank my drink and it was not long before I felt light headed. So I walked outside to get some air. There were a few people outside talking and smoking. So I walked over to the back of the property because there was a lake back there. I sat down on the ground, and I guess I fell asleep. But I felt someone touch me. I tried to scream, but there was a big hand over my mouth so I bit him. All of a sudden I felt something inside me. He was raping me. I went numb. I was a virgin. I was saving myself for marriage. It wasn't long, and he was done. I looked over at him and he looked familiar but I didn't know his name. I went home and took a shower, and never thought about it again. I was scared and embarrassed. I did not think anyone would believe me so I never said anything. I did not even know I was pregnant until I went into labor. I know it sounds crazy but I honestly did not know I was carrying you. When I went to the hospital I thought I was having just bad cramps. Well come to find out I was in labor. I had you, and the doctor asked me, if I wanted to hold you, and I told her no, because I knew you were a product of rape. I turned over and tried to sleep, but I heard you crying all night. I got up and left, I could not handle hearing you cry. I did walk past the nursery and you were the only baby in there and you were so beautiful. I looked down and you were crying and you happened to look my way and for one brief second you stopped crying. I walked out of the hospital because I was not able to take care of myself. I knew the hospital would place you. But If I would have known that they placed you with Seth and Millie I would have kept you. Honestly Kayla, I thought I was doing what was best for you."

"Patrice, I am sorry that you were raped but I need time to think" I say as I am walking to the door.

"Kayla, I will be right here when you are ready to talk. I love you Kayla and I hope that one day you will forgive me."

"I am sure I will, but right now I have to gather my thoughts. I do love you too."

I go to my room and lay on my bed and cry. I should have known that she had a horrible story. She is just like me. All these years I have wondered who my mother was. In a way if this was true and she is my mom it would be a dream come true. She has been the mother figure I never had and I did have an instant bond with her and felt more than a client relationship with her.

But where was she all those years? I get she was raped, but why not come take me away from Seth? Why not tell me that she was raped too? I thought we were more than patient and client. I thought we were friends.

I am so torn up, I don't know what to do with this. My heart is being pulled in several directions, and I can see why Garrett didn't want to tell me.

I am about to have a fucking nervous break-down when VI taps on the door and walks in.

"Girl, I saw Patrice and I overheard her call Rodney to arrange a DNA test. What the hell is going on? You look like you've seen a ghost."

I look up at her with tears running down my face and answer my best friend, "I just found out today that Patrice was raped by Seth and that I may be the child of rape. In fact they both are certain of it. The fucking bastard, who let me get raped for years and then threw me out with a check like some common whore could very well be my father. The woman I trusted for two years with everything is or could be my mother. So tell me what to do? VI, I have no fucking clue who I am. If it is true, I am a product of rape. My mother walked away from me because she was abused. The two people who were supposed to protect me didn't. So excuse me while I throw a pity party."

She runs over to me and wraps me in her arms.

"Oh fuck honey, no wonder you look like shit. What can I do? Do you want to talk or cry? Whatever you need I am here for you."

"No VI, I am done crying. I need to pull my shit together and go to talk to Garrett. And I need to apologize and make sure we are okay. I hope and pray that he can forgive me."

Just then he walks in the room.

"I am ok and we are more than ok baby. I am more worried about you and how you are holding up."

I run into his arms and just ask him to hold me because in his arms is the only place I feel safe and loved.

He picks me up carries me to bed and I lay in his arms

He tells me "If you are going to cry, let me be the one holding you while you do."

And the flood gates open again. I don't know how long we lay there but when I'm all cried out we go and take a hot bath.

"Babe, come here and let me just hold you." He says while we are in the bath tub.

"I'm so sorry."

"Babe, it's okay. I knew you were hurting and you lashed out. I should not have kept that from you. I swear I will never keep anything from you again."

"I know you didn't. I was just mad and upset."

"So did you and Patrice talk?"

"Well sort of. She told me that she was raped by Seth and I listened. When she was done, I walked out, but I did tell her I loved her."

"Honey, you learned some hard truths today and I know that you will have your faith to get you through this."

"Garrett, I know you are not a spiritual person, but will you pray with me?"

"Kayla, I'd move mountains if you asked."

So we say the only prayer that he knows.

Our Father in heaven, hallowed be your name.

Your Kingdom come, your will be done, on earth as in heaven

Give us today our daily bread.

Forgive us our sins, as we forgive those who sin against us.

Lead us not into temptation, but deliver us from evil.

For the kingdom, the power and the glory are yours.

Now and forever.

Amen.

"Thank you Garrett, I know that your spiritual side is not something you talk about a lot. But I want to thank you for praying with me."

"Honey I believe, but I was never taught how to pray. So please be patient with me and I will learn."

He bends down and slowly kisses me. I let out a soft moan.

"Kayla, if you keep making noises like those I will take you here and now."

"It wouldn't be the first time we have had sex in this tub babe." I reach down and stroke his already hard cock. I turn around and sit on his lap.

He kisses me on my collar bone and I let out a hiss as his teeth graze my skin. He bends his head down and grabs a nipple. He tugs on it with his teeth. I reach down and place him at my entrance, and with one swift thrust he is inside me. I close my eyes and slowly ride him.

"Babe, open your eyes!"

My eyes snap open, and I see the look on his face. I see the love that he has for me. I see the compassion.

I swivel my hips and bite his ear and that is all it takes. He grabs my shoulders and thrusts into me a few more times. I feel him tighten inside me and I know that he just released himself deep inside me.

He kisses the scars that line my body and whispers "You are so beautiful Kayla, and I love you so much."

I lay my head on his shoulder just enjoying his scent. I inhale and tell him, "I love you too."

We get out of the tub, and he towels me off. I grab my old, worn out jeans out of the closet with a coral shirt and matching flip-flops. After, I apply a touch of mascara and do a quick fishbone with my hair. Garrett laughs at me because I have on boxer briefs.

"Babe, do you own any girlie panties?"

"Yes I do but these are comfy, and I'm just at home. But if you want me to start wearing what you call girlie panties, then you need to buy me some."

"How about I give you my credit card, and you can pick them out?"

"Umm no, if you want me in sexy panties or lingerie, then you need to go and pick them out. And you can't take VI with you." I laugh.

"Not cool Kay, not cool at all. But since Christmas is right around the corner I will have to be thinking about your gifts."

"Oh hell, that is right. The holidays are right around the corner. The last few months have passed so fast, and I have had my head up my ass."

"Not true, you have had a trying time. Come on, let's go downstairs and see what everyone is doing. I am sure they are wondering what we are doing."

"Let them wonder. I am grown and this is my house." I lean over and kiss on his lips.

We go down stairs to find Wyatt cooking lunch.

VI and Patrice are talking.

VI is in her mother hen mode, and Wyatt is listing to them, asking a question here and there in his big brother mode.

"Patrice, all I want to know is if there is anything else that we need to know."

"No, I don't think so. I have told Kayla everything that I can remember."

"Okay you guys, I appreciate you all worrying about me. But I am grown and I can handle this. All my life I have wanted to know who my mother is, I now have a possible person. If Patrice is my mom, I will have some things to work through, but I will get through it. I do want to do the DNA test just for my sanity. No offense Patrice, but I don't want to take Seth's word."

"No dear, I didn't think you would. That is why I called Rodney and told him to run your blood against mine. I gave him a sample already so we will know soon."

"All I ask is that you all give me time. I am not asking for much. Just give me space."

They all shake their heads in agreement.

CHAPTER SEVEN
Chasing Dragons

"There comes a time when you have to choose between turning the page and closing the book."
~Unknown

I have started to go crazy waiting on the results. My dysfunctional family has gotten on my nerves. I love them dearly, but if they don't let me out of the house soon I may have to smother them in their sleep. Of course I won't, but they are pushing my buttons.

I have been counting down the days until I get the call. It has been four whole weeks since we sent off for the DNA results. I am pacing around the living room when my phone rings, it is an unknown number so I let it go to voicemail. I keep staring at my phone waiting on the notice that I have a voicemail. Within a few seconds I feel it vibrate. With shaking hands I hit the voicemail button, type in my code, and I hear the message. I know my life will change as soon as I hear the first words.

"This message is for Kayla Ashby, your results are in and we are 99.999997% that you are indeed the child of the alleged mother and alleged father."

I drop my phone and start crying. No one is in the room at that particular moment so I can cry in peace. But my peace does not last long because soon everyone is running toward me.

"Kayla honey, what is it." VI asks.

I glare up at her and she knows exactly what is wrong with me.

"I am not mad that she is my mom, at least I don't think I am. I am hurt, but I am not mad any longer.

I wanted a mom for so long and now I finally have one. But the fact that Seth is my father that is what is bothering me. He raped my mother, and here I am. I have no clue how I feel about that. I am thankful that my mother did not go the route of abortion, but how could she when she didn't even know she was pregnant. Seth on the other hand has always been a prick, and to thank I was raised by my real father all this time." I think to myself what will Millie think? She already hates me, maybe she has known this whole time, but why wouldn't she ever tell me, or tell Seth for that matter. I guess anyone can keep the paternity of her biological kids from their birth father, why wouldn't she do the same for me? She had to have known.

I go lay on my bed and pull out my journal from the bed side table. I will write out my thoughts because right now I really want to find a dealer.

Screw this. I slam the journal closed and gather my purse, my keys, and slip on my boots. I open my window and climb onto the fire-escape to the garage. I quietly unarm the beast and get in, fasten the seat beat and head out of the garage.

I hit the automatic dial feature on my console and ask to be connected to Damon. Within a few seconds I hear

""Yo! This is Damon."

"Damon, this is Kayla from Birmingham, and I need your hook up again."

"Birmingham, how have you been? I have not heard from you in a few months. Are you still in Seattle?"

"Yes Damon, I am. Can you please have someone meet me at the same place as before?"

"Birmingham, are you in some kind of trouble? You know people talk and there are rumors going around that you have some people that need to be taught a lesson."

"No Damon I am not okay, but I don't want anyone teaching any lessons, at least not right now. But thank you."

"No problem, you know I'd do anything for you Birmingham. So what are you looking for?"

"I'm looking for something to chase the dragon."

"Wow Birmingham, going for the hard stuff huh?"

"Yes, I am. I need a gram, and I want it pure. I have the cash. All I need to know is if you can get it to me? And how long will it take your guy to meet me."

"Birmingham, give me about ten minutes, and I will have someone meet you."

"Thank you Damon."

"You are welcome Birmingham, and I will call you right back and let you know if it will be the same guy on the motorcycle or not."

Okay, I'll be waiting. I'm coming off Pike Street, so let me know where."

"For sure."

I hit the end call button and it was silence once again in my beast.

I pull over off Everett and hit Hwy 99, which is the center for drugs and prostitution. I see hookers, drunks, and drug addicts everywhere. The buildings along the way are so run down and look like they could be crack houses. There are several pay by the hour motels that litter the street as well. There are pawn shops, and adult entertainment stores on every corner.

The bikini clad women are standing in the nasty, little espresso stands and prostitutes are on the street dressed provocatively and looking cheap and whorish. They all look like they have been rode hard and hung out wet.

My thoughts are disturbed by the sound of my phone ringing and I hit the answer button on my steering column.

"Birmingham, where are you?" Damon is asking.

"I am off Hwy 99 near the Boulevard Motel." I tell him as I am looking in the rearview mirror.

"Okay, pull into the back of the parking lot and Chase will meet you. He is the same guy as last time. He drives a black motorcycle. It will be one hundred and twenty bucks. I had him get some rigs as well because I was not sure if you had them."

"No I did not, thank you. I was not thinking when I made the call to you Damon."

"Well Chase will be there in just a few. Let me know if you need anything else."

"Damon, I know this sounds crazy but thank you."

"Birmingham, are you sure this is what you want to do? You know it has been seven years since you used. And I know how hard you worked on your sobriety."

"Damon, it is none of your business, no offense, but I am a grown ass woman and if I want to fuck up my life, then it is all on me. So thank you very much for getting me some *Brown Sugar,* but I really don't give a rat's ass on your opinion."

"Wow Birmingham, you must be dealing with some harsh shit because of all the years that we have known each other, you have never talked to me like that."

"I'm sorry Damon. Really I am, but I have had a really shitty day, and all I want is to forget."

"Okay, I get that, and I am so sorry. But he will be there in just a few minutes."

"Thank you, Damon."

"No problem, listen if you change your mind on that lesson please let me know. I will make a trip to Seattle if I need to."

"No, that is not necessary at the moment. And I will, I promise." I hit the end call button.

It doesn't take long and Chase is right beside me on his crotch rocket. Again, he is in all black. I see him casually get off his bike and stroll toward me. For a second I want to haul ass out of here, but instead I roll down my window.

"Birmingham?"

"Yep, that's me. Do you have what I am looking for? Pure uncut *Mexican Mud*."

"Yes, here is your Black Pearl and that will be one hundred and twenty bucks."

I hand him two hundred bucks and tell him to forget that he's ever seen me.

"No problem doll. If you ever need anything else, I can be reached at {206}-555-5577 and my name is Chase."

"First off, I am not your doll, and if I ever need anything again, I will go through Damon like I just did. Now if you will excuse me, I have something to do."

I roll up my window and decide that I am going to get a room for a little bit. I drive to the front of this flea bag motel and get out. I walk up to the window and see a sign that says *free condoms*. Wow! Really?

I ring the bell for service and it doesn't take long before an older Asian woman is walking over to the window.

"How long"

"Excuse me?" I ask.

"How long do you need the room?"

"Oh okay, for the night," I tell her. Her face lights up.

"That will be seventy five dollars."

I hand her eighty dollars and tell her to keep it.

She smiles and says "Room fourteen."

I don't even bother to say thank you. I simply walk out the door and go straight to room fourteen. I put the key in the door and open it. The room is small, but it is clean. Or at least it smells clean. I turn the television on for back ground noise.

I pull the drugs out of my purse and I am looking at them when my phone rings. I look at the caller ID and its Patrice's number that flashes across the screen.

I look down and see that I have missed eleven text messages. A few from Garrett, a few from VI, and even one from Rodney. I am sure by now they have discovered my Houdini act. I don't answer the phone and don't hit ignore. I know it won't take long for Rodney to find me.

My phone rings again and it's Damon, I immediately answer it thinking something is wrong with the goods that was just delivered to me.

CHAPTER EIGHT
The Longest Ride

"Whoever is happy will make others happy
too."
~Anne Frank

"Drop the needle Kayla," Rodney and Garrett
are screaming at me.

"Get out of my fucking room, and who are you
to tell me what the hell to do? You are not my daddy.
My dad is a man who raped my mother, and the last I
checked Rodney, you are not Seth Stanton."

"Kayla honey, please drop the needle. I love you
baby. Please look at me. We can get through this."

I glare at Garrett and tell him to leave me alone,
that he has nothing to do with this.

"Baby, please put down the dope and let me
have it. You can take your anger out on me. Please don't
lose your sobriety."

"What does it matter to you? You are not the
one who it will affect."

In the blink of an eye I am being tackled and the
dope knocked out of my hand.

"Get off me you ape! I can't breathe."

"It was the only choice I had. You can be pissed
at me all you want, but I will not apologize. I told you I
would protect you. Kayla, god damn it, why are you so
hard headed? You have a family. Let us help you, but
we can't do that unless you talk to us. We are not mind
readers. Now I will get off you, but you are going to get
your ass in the damn truck and we'll talk about this
when we are all home. Call it an intervention or

whatever you want, but I will not stand by and let you fuck up your life."

"I am not four Garrett. You can't make me get in the vehicle. Last time I checked, I was an adult. I am very capable of making up my own mind."

"Woman, I will not tell you again to get up and go get in the truck. If you don't I will go caveman and throw you over my shoulder and toss your ass in the truck. Now if you think I am playing, try me."

"You wouldn't dare."

"Okay, your choice." Garrett said

And before I can stop him he has me up and over his shoulder. My ass is in the air. I am beating him on his lower back, screaming for him to put me down.

Next thing I know I feel a slap on my ass and I scream. Not because it hurts but because I was shocked he did it.

"If you want to act like a child, I will treat you like a child. Children get their asses spanked when they are not listening so you have two choices, you can stop hitting me and act like the grown woman that you claim to be, or you can continue to act like a child. If you choose option two, then I will stop what I am doing and bend you over my knee and spank your ass."

As mad as I am at him I can't help but laugh at him.

"Put me down, please Garrett. I will be a good girl for now, but just know I am not happy with you."

"I know this and I can respect that, but you left me no choice."

"There is no need to be a smart ass Garrett. I said I would do as I am told for now. Don't think I will always be this obedient because it will be a cold day in hell. But for now I will do as you ask."

I get in his face, and point at him, "I will tell you this Garrett, I love you but I have issues, I am not perfect, and occasionally I will fuck up. So if you want to be with me you will need to know that I will slip. I have relapsed several times, and if you can't handle that, then we can call it quits now before either one of us hurts the other."

"Babe, I know you are not perfect. Hell we all have flaws, but we need to lean on each other when times are rocky. I am here, let me help you. I promise I am strong enough to help."

I glance around the room, and I see Rodney bagging up the dope and rigs and shaking his head.

"Kayla, do you know how worried your mom is about you?" Rodney asks.

I glare at him because I don't know if I will ever call her Mom. Me being a smart ass, I say "Patrice. It's Patrice. I can't call her mom."

"Just give her a chance. You know this is not just hard on you Kayla. She did what she thought was the best at the time. I know that she has been haunted as well. So when you are in your self-destruction phase, remember that you do have a mom that loves you. She may not have raised you, but I am sure giving you up was the hardest choice she ever made. So walk a mile in her shoes, and quit giving her shit."

"Rodney, you have no idea the hell I have lived. I was tortured and raped for years, and my biological father knew about it."

"Yes Kayla, I do have an idea. You need to remember I am a cop. I have seen some really bad shit over the years. And each time there is a victim, my heart breaks a little bit more. I am sorry for that but your mom, yes I said your mom, is hurting too. She just relived her rape and now she has a constant reminder. Guess who is her reminder? You are her reminder. So grab your big girl panties and stop being a brat because the pity train has derailed at the corner of it's time to Suck it up Street and Move on Avenue, and then crashed head into We all have problems Place and Time to get the hell over it Boulevard. Hell Kayla I have an aunt, her name is Sheila, and guess what? She is blind and paralyzed and she doesn't have a pity party. She lives in the dark every damn day and she is scared of the dark. And what are you doing? You're sitting here crying because you don't like your birth parents. Well wake up sweetheart. You don't get to choose your damn parents. No one likes their damn parents. Hell I am sure Garrett didn't like his either, but you don't hear him crying. So I am going to say this one-time and one-time only, you want me to treat you like you're an adult, then you damn sure better act your age and not you're fucking shoe size"

I look at both men in this room and I know that they are speaking the truth. Hell Rodney doesn't even know me and he is speaking the truth. So I walk over and grab my purse and walk out the door.

A few seconds later I hear the footsteps of them behind me.

"Garrett, you take Kayla's truck back and she can ride with me.

"No I can drive myself. I am not a child."

"Kayla, I am not asking. I can be an ass and take you to jail. So ride with me voluntarily or you ride in the back with cuffs on."

I look at him stunned. "Are you serious Rodney? You would arrest me?"

"I am very serious Kayla. You could be charged with a controlled substance and drug paraphernalia, which can result in one year in prison and up to a five thousand dollar fine. Do you really want to take that chance and see if I will arrest you? Because I promise I will have no problems arresting you."

"First off Rodney, you guys kicked in my door. Did you have probable cause? A warrant? No, I never saw a warrant. You can't use the drugs as evidence because guess what, you have violated my 4th amendment rights."

The look of shock is written all over his face.

"Oh didn't you know? I was pre law before I changed majors and became an architect. So if you are going to spit the law at me, I guess your ass better make sure that you are on the right side of it. I do believe what you guys did was an unlawful entry and guess what, you can't do jack shit, but just for shits and giggles I will go with you, not because you are making me, but because I am not in the mood to argue with you any longer."

"Babe, I will see you at the house."

"Okay, see you there. I love you."

"I love you too babe, and please listen to him. He's only trying to help you. He loves your mom, or Patrice as you are calling her. Think about her during all this. I am sure it's twice as hard on her."

He leans down and kisses me on the forehead.

"Come on Kayla, we need to talk." Rodney states.

"Okay, so what do you want to talk about Rodney?"

"Well first off, I think you owe Patrice an apology. She was scared shitless. She had went into your room and you were gone. She was coming down the stairs panicking when Garrett got the call from your friend Damon."

"He's not my friend. More like a frenemy."

"Anyway, whatever he is, his phone call most likely saved Seth's ass because she was sure that someone had taken you."

"Rodney, I know you are only looking out for Patrice, but I really don't owe anyone anything." I cross my hands over chest and let out a loud breath.

"I'm sorry that you feel that way. Because regardless what you think, Patrice loves you and she is hurting just as much if not more than you are."

"How in the hell do you figure that Ace?"

"She has felt guilty for over twenty-five years. When she walked out of that hospital, she had the best of intentions. She wanted what was best for you. Do you think she would have packed up and flew across the damn country for just anyone? No, she has a bond with you. There was something inside her telling her that she could help you. And why you do you think that is?"

I shrug my shoulders and gaze out the window and watch Seattle pass us by.

"Kayla, you are not dumb. I know that you feel the same bond she does. She loves you and I know deep down you love her too. Yes, you have a right to be upset, but have a little compassion for her. She is hurting just like you. So if you can't find in your heart to show her you care enough to simply apologize for acting like a spoiled brat who didn't get a pony for her birthday, then you need to tell her to go home. She deserves a chance Kayla."

"Rodney, I will think about it, okay? That is the best answer I can give you right now. I will be civil and respectful of Patrice. I can't offer anything else right now. I am sorry. "

"All I ask is that you try. Walk in her shoes for just a minute. Imagine giving up a child then finding out that the child you gave up was raised by monsters. Don't you think she has enough guilt?"

With that, I get out of the police car and I see the beast parked in her spot so I know Garrett is home.

"I will be up in a minute, Rodney."

"Kayla no offense but can I have your purse? "

"You know, I'm too tired to even argue with you. I only want to gather my thoughts before I walk into my house, but if it'll make you feel better, take my damn purse. You won't find anything else. Hell, you already have all the damn dope."

"Kayla, believe me when I say I don't want to be the hard ass. I have really grown to like you. You remind me of myself when I was younger—stubborn and very hard headed but in the end you will do what is best."

"I'll be up in a few. Please allow me to stand here and look at the Seattle skyline."

He nods his head and hits the elevator button. I hear it ding and then going up.

I walk over to the edge of the parking garage and see the city of Seattle. It is around eleven at night so there is a brisk breeze blowing in the air. This city is so impressive at night.

In the distance I can hear the soft music coming from one of the many organs at St. James Cathedral. I catch myself walking in that direction. The soft music is soothing. It doesn't take long before I am standing outside the massive doors. I walk up the steps and pull open the big wooden slabs. It feels like a higher power is gliding me across the black and white checkered floor. I see all the candles that have been lit for those who are needing prayers. I stop and light one not really knowing who I am praying for, but it just feels right.

I dip my hand in holy water and place a cross across my body.

I make my way to the front of the church. I look up and see all the beautiful stained glass. Each one cascades a different light.

The lights are dim and it's creating a soft glow around the cross.

We are in the season of Advent so the reds and gold's are perfect shades.

Up in the choir loft I hear the sweet sound of Christmas music, and I know immediately that it is the children's chorus. They are singing *Oh Holy Night*, which is my all-time favorite Christmas Carol.

I make my way to the third row which is the one I always sit at. I pull down the small bench under the pews for prayers.

It is not long and I feel at peace. I get back up in the pew and just think about my life and where it is going. Can I actually have a relationship with her? Could I do what she did? Have a baby and just walk away? I know she had her reasons, but why not tell me as soon as she suspected? Was there ever a clue? I have asked myself who am I?

I close my eyes and I pray. I say a prayer that I used to say when I was trying to kick my old habits.

Lord,

I commit my failures, as well as my successes into your hands, and I bring for your healing the people and the situations, the wrongs and the hurts of the past. Give me courage, strength, and generosity to let go and move on—

leaving the past behind me, and living the present to the full. Lead me always to be positive as I entrust the past to your mercy, the present to your love, and the future to your providence.

> *In your name I pray,*
> *Amen*

I guess I nod off because the next thing I know, I wake up and Patrice is right beside me. She has tears in her eyes.

"Kayla, I understand if you don't want to talk to me, but if you will listen to what I have to say, then I will leave you alone. Will you at least listen to me?"

"Yes, I will." I wipe a tear off my face and she grabs my hand, and I don't pull away.

"Kayla, can I tell you about my past and then you can make your choice?"

I nod my head yes.

"I was raised dirt poor. My dad was lower class and did not have a pot to piss in. He was a good man when he was not in a chemically induced state. He was much like you when I first met you, I swore that you looked just like him. My father had a lot of problems. I was told that he was a manic depressant and was bipolar. But he also had a drug problem. His drug of choice was Meth or some street terms that you would know are crank, chalk or speed. When he was high, he was meaner than a rattlesnake. He would say hateful things. I remember one night he was so messed up that he made me undress and stand in the kitchen on a bed of rice, because he thought I had lied about where my mom was."

"You see my mom passed away shortly after I was born. Everyone says that she died from complications of child birth. I have no memories of her at all. I stayed with my grandmother the majority of the time. She did her best but she was aging and when she passed I had no choice but to live with him. When I was a teenager and had my fill of the verbal abuse, I left. I did not have two wooden nickels to rub together, so I knew I would not get far without an education and money. So what kind of job can a woman find with no experience? I took the first job I could get. I am not proud of it. I was a stripper. My stage name was Phoenix. I made good money and before long I had an apartment. For the first time in my life I was truly living. I was enrolled in college and I was doing really well in school. I was one semester away from getting my degree in Psychology."

"I went into work one Friday evening and a friend of mine named, Rayna, said that there was a party and we needed to go. They were paying top dollar for a couple of girls to dance for some frat guys. So I agreed and went to the frat house. It was loud and the guys were already drinking heavily. Of course I didn't care that they were drinking, I was there to make money and leave. After our dance was over, I went up to the bar area and asked for a Sprite. There was no alcohol in the drink at all. Or at least there was not supposed to be. But now that I think about it, there was most likely vodka in the cup. It's clear and has no smell. So I drank half of it and had to go the restroom. I was only there for maybe a minute and I had asked Rayna to watch my drink. When I came back she was talking to Seth, I had seen him around campus before, but I never talked to him, so we all talked for a few minutes and everything was going good. He seemed so nice. He was good looking. I had noticed he had a white ring around his ring finger. I even asked him if his Wifey had let him off the ball and chain tonight. He of course laughed and said something like that."

"I excused myself because I needed some air as the room was starting to spin. I thought it was just because there was so many people and the music was really loud. So I walked outside with no direction in mind. I was just wandering and I spotted the water at the back. I have always been mesmerized by water at night. I started feeling really tired, so I took off my jacket and sat down on it not thinking I would fall asleep. But I did. I remember hearing voices, I knew there were several people around. I kept trying to open my eyes but it was like they were glued shut. But all of a sudden there was someone on top of me. His voice was so familiar. I had just heard it. I remember him saying you are not the one I was planning on but you will work."

"He held me down and had his hand over my mouth. I remember biting his hand. That did not even phase him. He kept telling me what a lucky woman I was because he could have any woman he wanted. When he finally finished, he got up and walked away. I laid there for a few minutes because I was embarrassed. When I did leave, I went back to my apartment, took a scalding hot shower, and then packed up all my stuff and left. I got in my car and headed to Texas, and I've lived there ever since. I had all my schooling transferred to Baylor College and finished there. I got my degree in Psychology. I also have a practice in Birmingham and that is where I met you."

"When you were born I did not even name you so you were given a name by a nurse. I do have your hospital bracelet that I had on and it said baby girl as your name. I am so sorry that you had a hard and rough life. Believe me if I could have traded places with you, I would in a minute. I hope you can forgive me one day."

Patrice begins to get up, but I stop her.

"I'm sorry I scared you. Can you ever forgive me Mom?"

"Oh honey, there is nothing to forgive."

We are both crying. And she whispers I love you.

"I love you too, mom. Now can we please go home? I am sure Garrett is going out of his mind. Oh, how did you know where I was?"

"I followed you. I knew you would not come right up, and I was right. What made you come to this church?"

"I don't know. I heard the soothing music, and I just love it here."

"Me too dear. Me too."

CHAPTER NINE

Dealing with Life

"Forget what hurt you, but never forget what it
taught you."
~Unknown

It has been two long weeks since we got the
DNA test back. Patrice is my mother, and we are
working on our relationship. It is weird, but we are both
trying.

Seth tried calling my cell when he got his copy
of the DNA test. I didn't even bother answering it. I
don't want to hear a word that prick has to say. As far as
I am concerned, he can go to the seventh circle of hell
and burn to death, for all I care.

Garrett and I were in bed later that night and he
was holding me after a hot session of love making. We
were talking while I am laying on his chest, and he rubs
my back

"So how do you feel now that everything is now
out in the open?"

"I am glad Patrice is my mom, but it still sucks
ass that the prick is my dad. But I don't want to think
about him after the mind blowing sex. I just know as
long as I have you I will make it through anything."

"You will never lose me. I will be here forever."

"I love you Garrett."

"I love you too Kayla."

We fall asleep in each other's arms, but
sometime later I wake up screaming.

"Kay honey, are you okay?"

"Don't touch me. Get away."

"Kayla, it's me Garrett."

"Please don't hurt me. I am begging you."

"Please don't push me away. I will not hurt you Kayla. Come talk to me. What is going on? Was it a nightmare?"

I look up and notice I am at home and not back at the pool house. I am crying and shaking. I get up and run to the bathroom and slam the door shut and lock it. Seconds later I hear Garrett.

"Kay, please talk to me. What is going on?"

I ignore him and turn on the hot shower and I strip.

I stand in the shower and I cry. I have not had a nightmare in a long time, but this one was bad. I scrub my body trying my best to get their scent off me. I know in my head it was only a harsh nightmare but my body is telling me it was real. I hate them.

I sit on the bench and cry until the water turns cold, and even then I still sit and cry.

I finally turn off the water and look at myself in the mirror. I look at the bright red scars. I run my fingers along the jagged edges. The scars are a constant reminder of my past. I grab the fluffy robe and head to the door. I open it and see the whole family in my room.

I don't even get out of the room, and I am being bombarded with questions.

I shake my head at VI, and she knows to get everyone out.

It's not long before it's just VI and I. She sits there waiting on me to say something first.

"This one was really bad," I whisper.

"Do you want to tell me about it?"

"Not really. I just want to sit here. Will you brush my hair like you used to when we were younger? It was always so calming."

"Absolutely, give me the brush and go sit at the vanity."

"Will you tell me about you and Wyatt? Tell me something to get my mind off the nightmare."

"Hmmm, what to tell. He is this super romantic guy. He holds me at night like he is afraid I will not be there in the morning. But sometimes he will say her name."

"Whose name?"

"Ariel. You know, his wildflower."

"What does he say?"

"Nothing really, but I can tell he really loved her. She did a number on him. She left and never looked back. I met her once back in college. She was nice and she was gorgeous. He has a picture of her in his wallet. It's old and bent, but it's still there. Before you go all saintly on me, he showed me her one night. He was wasted. I had to go to the club and pick him up. Girl he was shit faced."

"When was this? And why didn't I know about it?"

"Well it was as soon as he was released from the hospital. You were still in the coma, and he went to the club and got drunk. When I walked in the door, the place was destroyed. He had taken a baseball bat and destroyed his office. He was so upset."

"Why? It was not his fault. It was mine."

"Kay, don't you know those men love you. Both Garrett and Wyatt love you more than all the words in all the books in the world."

"Wow that's a lot of love. I think I hurt Garrett's feelings tonight though. I screamed for him not to touch me. And then I got up and ran to the bathroom and locked him out."

"Oh Kay, he understands."

"He has understood a lot here lately and I can't keep asking him to understand. You should have seen his face when I had the needle in my hand and he tackled me. VI, he was scared shitless."

"Speaking of that night, what the fuck were you thinking?"

"I wasn't. Plain and simple. I was not thinking about anything or anyone. I heard that message and my heart stopped and I just wanted to numb the pain. That was the only way I knew how to do it."

"So this Damon fellow, have you talked to him?"

"No, I have not. I did send him a message telling him that I was okay. He has messaged me several times checking on me but I have not responded to any of them. I am thankful that he called but I am mad as hell at him. He had no right."

"No Kay, he did not, but your family is glad he did. You should have seen Garrett when he got the call. He was scared that Rodney wouldn't make it in time. He didn't give a Rodney a chance to tell him that he could not go. He was out the door and getting in Rodney's car."

"That night was a nightmare and I owe you an apology."

"Me? Why do you owe me an apology? Kay, you are grown. No-one can make decisions for you. Do I approve? Hell no, but do I think you owe me an apology? No ma'am I don't. I know things have been difficult for you."

"That is an understatement."

"Come on lets go tell the family that you are okay, so they can quit pacing. I can hear them from here."

"Do I have to go down there? I really made an ass of myself."

"Yes, you have to, but luckily for you, we all love your ass, so you will be fine. So get dressed and let's go have some coffee, since the whole house is wide awake at freakin four am. Maybe we can get lucky and there is breakfast made."

"I will be down in a few. Let me get dressed."

"Okay gutterslut, love your face."

"Love your face more."

"I doubt that, but I will let you think you won."

Soon I am alone with my thoughts. I walk over to my double French doors that lead to my custom patio. I open the doors and there is a subtle breeze. I walk out and look over the city. The Seattle skyline never looked better. To the left of me is the ever impressive Seattle Space Needle. In the distance I can see the snow-capped mountains of Mt. Rainier. I am close enough to the water that I can watch the ferries pass. Down below me is Pike Place market, where crowds gather to watch the fisherman throw salmon.

Seattle is a posh mosh of head-spinning whirlwind of just everything you can ever want. To the right of me, I see the twinkling lights of downtown. I can see the big Ferris wheel. I look over my patio and I see the large red oak chairs and the massive table tucked in the corner I have my own piece of heaven, I have my atrium. I have everything from my favorite white roses that have pink edges to my butterfly plants that bring in butterflies. I have a Peperomia which adds a splash of color. I have a Chinese Ever-green that has shades of silver and gray and several varieties of Ivy. I have a Dracaena which looks like a cornstalk. I have several snake plants, spider plants, a Boston fern that is virtually indestructible. I even have a Crown of Thorns plant, and in the center I have a stone water feature. I had it custom built. It is in the shape of a cross and the water flows up the cross instead of down. I have a stone pathway leading back to the French Double doors. I look over and I see Garrett staring at me.

"Are you okay?"

"Yes I am fine. I'm sorry. I thought you were Elijah. I was having a very bad nightmare."

"Do you want to talk about it?"

"No I don't. Garrett, are you sure you want to be with me? I'm toxic. I don't want to hold you back from someone who could be better than me."

"There is no one who could ever be better than you. I mean it when I say you are the one I want."

I run to him and start crying in his shoulder. "I just don't want you to have to settle."

"There is no settling. I promise. I wouldn't have been settling with anyone else."

"I'm tired. Can you please lay with me until I fall asleep?"

"Of course. "

We get back into the bed and it doesn't take long for us to fall asleep.

***

"Seth you have been pacing this house for two weeks. What in the hell is going on?"

"What did you ask Millie? I am sorry, my mind is elsewhere right now."

"Yeah, no shit. You have not even said five words to me since the funeral. And thank you for causing a scene at Edwin's funeral. How did Jason even find out? Now he is threatening me with lawsuits because I kept the boys from him."

"Millie, I don't know how he found out, but you did tell a room full of people your sad story at the hospital."

"I bet it was the little gold digging bitch Kayla."

"Don't you dare call her that? You have caused her enough shit. Leave her alone."

"Wow Seth, when did you start caring for the little trollop?"

I walk over to Millie, and got in her face and tell her to back the fuck off. "Leave her alone. She is none of your concern."

"Oh bull shit Seth, she killed my son. Don't tell me that she is not my concern. All this time you have raised Edwin and Elijah as your kids, and you are taking her side. Have you lost your mind?"

"Millie I am not going to have this conversation with you. I am warning you, if you don't back off, you will regret it."

"Is that a threat Seth? As I told that whore in the hospital, I don't deal well with threats."

I reach over and slap her across the face, "I told you to shut the fuck up. Drop your hatred for Kayla now. I will not have this conversation again."

She grabs her cheek and gets to the door. "Seth I have covered your ass for years and you can't even do one thing for me. That is okay. I got you."

She slams the door and the windows rattle.

I try to call Kayla several times. I need to talk to her. I need her to know how sorry I am. Of course, no answer.

I leave her a message. Telling her it's urgent. I try Patrice.

"This is Dr. Doyle, how can I help you?"

"Patrice, this is Seth, Please don't hang up. I need to talk to Kayla."

"Good luck with that Seth. She wants nothing to do with you. You raised her all these years, and you let those monsters rape her. They may not be yours by blood, but they are just like you."

All of a sudden the line goes dead.

CHAPTER TEN
The Holiday Brings Stress

"Only you can control your future."
~Dr. Seuss

"I can't believe it is already Thanksgiving. I have never had a real family dinner. So this year I am going to cook. Lord help me. Mom, can you make me a list of things I need from the store?"

"You're serious? You want to cook?"

"Yes. Why are you guys laughing?"

"None of us have seen you in the kitchen other than to grab some wine or to eat the food someone else prepared."

"You guys can joke all you want."

"Do you have any idea how to cook? Do you think you can prepare something like Thanksgiving dinner?"

"Well, I have Googled it and watched You Tube. How hard can it be?"

"Kayla sweetheart, I can cook the meal. Well, we can order a fried turkey, and then I can make the rest."

"You guys, will you please trust me? This is something I want to do so please shush and make me a list. We only have a few days before Thanksgiving, so I need to get my turkey now. Please write down everything I'll need. I need to get to the store."

"Well, can you tell me what you want to make?"

"Hello, I just told you guys I have never had a real Thanksgiving dinner."

"Wait, Seth and Millie never fixed holiday meals?" VI asks.

"Nope, never. They were always out of town for the holidays. The help always made seafood for the holidays. That's why I'm asking for a list. I have no clue what I need to buy."

"Come on buttercup. There's no need for a list. You and I will go shopping." Wyatt said.

"I'll let the name slide you ass, but only because you are taking me shopping. Let me grab my purse and then we can be on our way."

"Who all is going?" Wyatt asks.

"Just you and me stud. Come on."

"Hey now! You have a man. Don't be flirting with mine." VI says, laughing.

"Oh VI, your man couldn't handle this." I run my hands down my side laughing.

"Kayla babe, you would be ruined for any other man." Wyatt joked.

"Brother, if you were anyone else I'd knock you out, but seeing how we are blood, I'll let you live." Garrett laughs.

"Come on Wyatt. I want to go before all the fat turkeys are gone."

"Oh hell, I better go."

"Let's drive the beast, but you can't touch my radio stations Wyatt, and I mean it."

"There better not be country blaring in my ears."

"Just for that smart ass, I will make sure of it."

I grab him and pull him to the door. I grab my keys, my pink Coach purse, and put my Gucci sunglasses on before heading out the door.

We get to the beast and I hit the alarm to unlock the doors. I get inside and push the button to start the car. I fasten my seatbelt and turn the radio on. I'm greeted by Meghan Trainor's *Lips are Moving*.

"Aw Buttercup, this is not the good music, but this is an improvement. You're may finally be moving up in the music world."

Ignoring his comment, I ask, "Okay so what store are we buying out?"

"The only one I shop at—PCC Natural Markets."

"Okay, let's go do some damage."

We are only a few minutes away so we make small talk until we arrive at the store. I have never shopped with Wyatt and he will soon find out that shopping is an excursion with me because I go down every single isle.

A while later, Wyatt says, "Kayla, are you serious? We have everything already."

"Oh hush cry baby. We have only been here for over an hour. But you're right, I think we have everything on our list." I grabbed the biggest turkey I could find. It's a beast at 23 pounds.

We get up to the register, and she rings everything up and gives me the grand total of three hundred twenty seven dollars.

"Kayla, have you lost your damn mind? Its only one dinner!"

"Yes but it's my first family dinner. So like you tell me, suck it up buttercup. Now load those groceries so we can head back to the house because I am excited to start baking."

"Oh God! I just know you're going to burn your house down." Wyatt groans.

"Well if I burn the house down, I can design a new one."

"Ooh, well played Buttercup!"

***

Over the next few days, I search every cooking website I can think of because I want to show them that I can do this.

I have made several pies—Dutch apple, spicy pumpkin, and a southern pecan pie. I am standing in my kitchen, and I have flour everywhere when Garrett walks in and starts laughing at me.

"I should so record this because you may never cook another meal again."

"Ha-Ha, very funny. I am trying here."

"It smells good in here—smells like a bakery."

"All I can say is I am trying and if it doesn't turn out, there's always Chinese."

"I am really proud of you. I have never seen you in the kitchen, and I find it really sexy."

He comes over and wipes some flour off my nose and gently kisses my forehead. "I will let you butter my buns later."

"Is that a promise?"

"Yes it is."

"What is your favorite thing about Thanksgiving?"

"Oh wow, as a man I know I am supposed to say football but I love the food. So don't mess up my favorite part."

"It's not like I didn't have enough pressure. Thanks for adding to it, Asshat! Anyways how is work? Sign any one new lately?"

"I am working on signing this new and up-coming author, but I can't discuss anything. She is pretty kick ass, though. I am excited."

"Yay! I hope you sign her! How is your mom?"

"She is good. I think they are in Europe right now. Wyatt invited her for Thanksgiving, but she said they were not going to be here. I know what the answer to this will be, but I'm going to ask anyway. Have you talked to Seth?"

"No I have not. He has called me several times and sent me lots of texts messages, but as far as me actually listening to him, the answer is no. As far as I am concerned, he can go fuck himself."

"Kay, isn't that a little harsh? He is your father. Don't you think you should hear him out?"

"Garrett, you are walking on very thin ice. I have nothing to say to him. One day maybe I will forgive him, but that day is not going to be today."

"Okay, I won't bring it up again. I was just asking love."

"Yes I know and thank you, but right now he's a sore subject for me."

"I get it. I don't agree with you, but I get it."

"Garrett, you hated your father. He beat you, your brother, and mom. So you mean to tell me if he was alive that you would have something to do with him?"

"You talk about your faith all the time Kay. How is it you can have faith in some things but not others? I am an adult now, so yes I would try to have a relationship with my father. Remember babe, tomorrow is not promised to anyone."

"I am done with this conversation. I have food to prepare so if you are going to keep giving me shit, please leave the kitchen."

I watch him get up and leave. I turn and face the window by the sink, and I can't help but break down.

I take off my apron and throw it on the granite counter. I grab my keys and walk out the door. I have no destination in mind, but I know I have to get out of the house. I get in the beast and just start driving. I drive for a few minutes, and I end up at Seattle's Great Wheel.

I have never been here, but it looks like a great place to just sit and think. There is a park bench right out front, and I walk over and take a seat. I watch the kids — their little faces light up when seeing the great wheel for the first time. I watch the lovers strolling along, hand-in-hand and an older couple who look like they have weathered many storms together. They are sitting so close that they look like one. She lovingly looks up at her partner, and he gently kisses her cheek. I watch as they get up and dance. There is no music around, but they are in perfect harmony. I notice that he never lets her hand go. He holds her like she is his reason for breathing. You can tell that he loves her unconditionally.

I sit there for a few more minutes and I see a man and a little girl. She can't be more than five or six. She has on a white flowered dress and has her hair in braids. He has on slacks and nice dress shirt. She is crying and it looks like she hurt her knee. He has bent down and picked her up. He walks over to a table and sits her down. He gets down on one knee and examines her knee. He gives it a kiss, and she stops crying. Just like that...one little kiss and she was over her pain. *Is it really that simple? Can a father's love really be like that?*

I know what I have to do. I have to forgive him — Garrett was right. My faith needs to be overall, not just one sided.

I get back in the beast and head home. I look at the clock, and I have been gone for a few hours. I left without my phone, so I am sure there will be an APB out for me.

I get home and there is no one there. So I go straight to bed. It has been a long day and I am exhausted.

***

Thanksgiving Day is finally here, and I find myself up before everyone else. I had the turkey in the oven before five that morning, and I have all the sides made and the table set. The only thing I'm waiting on is the turkey to be finished. Everyone else is in the living room watching football, and I can hear them yelling about a play.

I love hearing them laugh.

I look over and Rodney is walking into the kitchen for another beer.

"Hey Kayla, how are you today?"

"I am good and you?"

"I am starving. That bird needs to hurry up. I think my stomach is touching my back."

I look at him and laugh because he doesn't look like he has ever missed a meal.

"Kayla, don't let this belly fool you. It's hard work keeping this shape."

"You're such a mess, but I see why my mom is crushing on you. You're one of the good guys."

"Can I tell you a secret?"

"Well sure Rodney."

"I'm kind of crushing on her as well."

"I knew it. I can see the way you look at her."

We are interrupted when the oven timer goes off. The turkey is done!

Rodney's eyes light up, "Let me get that out of the oven for you."

"Fingers crossed it is done because if it is not, we will be eating Chinese."

"Oh God I hope not. My mouth is watering just from smelling this bird in the oven."

Rodney takes the turkey out of the oven, and I put it on the platter.

"Rodney will you do the honors of cutting the turkey?"

"I'd be honored. Of course that means I get to taste it first, right?"

"Sure, that way if it's not good, you can tell me."

"It will be fine. Look at this Kayla, this is a beautiful bird."

I yell for everyone to come and eat.

We gather around the table and I say a prayer.

O Gracious God, we give you thanks for your overflowing generosity to us. Thank you for the blessings of the food we eat and especially for this feast today. Thank you for our home and family and friends, especially for the presence of those gathered here. Thank you for our health, our work and our play. Please send help to those who are hungry, alone, sick and suffering war and violence. Open our hearts to your love. We ask your blessing through Christ your son. Amen.

Dinner was a hit. Everyone has a belly full of food and we are sitting around enjoying each other's company when Rodney's phone rings.

"Excuse me, it's the station."

We make small talk for a few minutes and when Rodney walks back in, I can see something is wrong.

Patrice walks up to him and grabs his hand, "Honey, what is wrong?"

"It's Elijah. He was released from the hospital."

CHAPTER ELEVEN
The Plan

"There's a terrible price to pay for stress in your
life - it really takes a hit on your heart."
~Leeza Gibbons

My world stops when I hear Elijah has been
released. I go into complete panic mode.

"Kayla, I will make sure there are extra cops
patrolling this area."

"It won't make a difference. He will make me
pay. He is going to be worse now after his brother
dying. Edwin was actually less evil than Elijah. At least
Edwin had half a heart. Elijah is outright cold and he
doesn't care about going to jail. Can't you see it doesn't
scare him?

"I promise, you will be safe."

"Rodney, no offense, but you can't promise that,
so please don't make promises you can't keep."

"Well, I can do my best, but for now, no more
outings on your own."

"I'm sorry, but there is no way in hell I'm going
to stay locked inside. It doesn't matter where I am or if
I'm alone or in a crowd. He wants me and he'll make it
happen. He is a snake and will strike when and where
he wants.

"Is there anything we can do, Rodney?" Patrice
asks.

"All I can offer is make sure you watch your
surroundings. Patrice, I don't think he knows anything
about you, but please keep your eyes open. VI, Wyatt,
and Garrett, you know he already has it out for y'all. So

my advice is to stay home. Don't go out shopping for Black Friday."

"I'm sorry Rodney, but I will not miss shopping because of him. I have plans tomorrow, and he can kiss my ass."

"Kayla, what plans do you have?" Garrett asks.

"I'm buying all your Christmas gifts, and none of you are coming with me. I will take VI's Taser."

"Kayla, did you not just hear what Rodney said?"

"Yeah I heard Mom, but I have plans. I will check in every hour. Don't worry. I will be fine. I am tired of living in fear. I looked over my shoulder for seven long years, and I refuse to do it any longer. This is not open for discussion."

I walk out of the dining room because I am done. I head down the hallway and go to my room. I walk across the floor to the double doors and out to my patio taking a seat on the dark chocolate chaise lounge. This is my thinking spot. I have to come up with a plan to deal with Elijah because if he isn't dealt with, this nightmare will keep repeating—kind of like the movie Groundhog's Day.

My thoughts are interrupted by VI.

"Kay, I see the wheels in your head turning. You are practically smoking out of your ears. So tell me your plan because I know you are forming one. If I need to be an alibi I will."

"VI, you know me too well, but I will not let you or anyone be an accessory to my crime or crimes."

"Kayla, I am not asking. You either tell me, or you don't get to leave without me. I am not playing. You remember what happened last time you didn't let me in on your plan."

"Well, last time there was no plan. You ma'am went in there half-cocked. I just refused to wait on back up."

"Do you want me to go and get Wyatt and Garrett, or Rodney for that matter? Because I will."

I pull her arm back and tell her, "No, I don't want that, but I seriously don't have a plan—just an idea."

"Okay, so spill it sis. I am not playing."

"Okay, so I am going to make a call to Damon. He has told me he can come and teach someone a lesson."

"Okay so make the call now. I want to hear what your plan is."

"Dang you are pushy."

"No, I am being protective."

I grab my phone from my bra, and I dial his number

"Yo, this is Damon."

"Damon, this is Birmingham."

"Birmingham, are you okay?"

"Yeah, I'm fine, but this is not a social call. I need your help."

"Okay, but I'm telling you I'm not selling you anything ever again."

"No, this has nothing to do with that."

"Okay, so tell me what it is you need."

"The last time we talked, you said you would come and teach someone a lesson for me. I need to call in that favor now."

"Okay, when do you need this done?"

"I need it done like now. I'll pay for your flight out here and pay you whatever you ask for when it's done."

"Okay, when you say done, do you mean like done-done?"

"No. Here's my plan. I need your goons to beat up someone and torture him for six hours."

"Okay, I can do that. Give me an hour to get to the airport. I will be traveling with two men."

"Okay, three first class flights are being booked right now."

VI nods her head and get on the computer.

"Will you need transportation and lodging while you're here?"

"No Birmingham, I can handle all that."

"Okay deal, but I have one more favor and I know you said no, but can you get a rig when you get here?"

"Do I want to know what for?"

"No, you don't. The less I tell you, the better off you are."

"Okay, I'll let you know when I land."

"Thank you Damon, for everything. Oh, and I'm sorry about the other day."

"No worries. I just hope I got them there in time."

"Yes, you did, but barely."

The phone disconnects, and I know our conversation is over.

"Are you sure about this, Kay?"

"Yes, I am ready for this shit to be over, but I do need your help with one more thing."

"Okay, name it and I'll do what I can."

I need you to go shopping for me because I can't come back with no presents. I want you to take my card and buy for everyone. We also need a Christmas tree and decorations. I want you to meet me at Northgate Mall in the food court at four pm."

"Is there something you're not telling me, Kay?"

I smile at her, and she knows I am hiding something.

"I told you I won't tell you everything because I don't want you to know how evil I really am. Now go get some sleep and be ready to leave at five am."

"Holy hell! Are you out of your fucking mind? That's before the chickens even get up."

"Well, I can leave you here."

"No, no that isn't necessary. I'll be ready. We will need to stop by Starbucks first thing."

"I can handle that."

My phone rings, and I see its Damon.

"Hello Damon."

"Hey Birmingham. We are headed to the airport."

"Okay, your tickets are there. Talk to you soon."

"For sure."

The call ends again.

"Go to bed VI. I love your face."

"I love yours too."

She gets up and leaves the patio. I follow and walk over to my closet and pick out my clothes. I choose a pair of old jeans, a tank top, and an old sweater. I grab my tennis shoes, jacket, and my black knock off purse. I lay them on the chair by the vanity.

Garrett walks in and sees that I have clothes laid out.

"You're serious? You're really going shopping?"

"Yes Garrett, I am. VI is going with me, so calm down. We're leaving at five in the morning."

"I can't believe that you are going to do this. He has already hurt both of you once."

"Garrett, I can't live my life in fear any longer. I've lived that life and I am over it."

"Kayla, you're insane. Why go out looking for trouble?"

"Would it be better that he come here and hurt me in my own house? I don't think so, Garrett. I am over my fear of him. He can't hurt me anymore."

"How do you figure? He can kill you, and you know as well as I do, he will do it if he has the chance."

"I'm not going to stay cooped up. I'm sorry, but this is not open for discussion."

"You're hiding something. You're too calm."

"I am hiding nothing, Garrett. I am going shopping. I have a home to decorate for Christmas. Tomorrow is the biggest shopping day of the year. I have not missed a Black Friday sale since I was sixteen, and I will not miss this one."

"I don't understand you. I don't see your logic."

"I'm asking you to have faith in me. It will all work out."

"I can see that I'm not going to win this battle."

I tap him on the shoulder and tell him, "No babe, you're not. Let's go to bed. I'm tired, and I have to get up in a few hours because I have a dent to put in my credit card."

"Okay, let's go to bed."

We get into bed, and I lay on my side with Garrett behind me. I can feel his erection forming, so I stick my ass out further and hear him hiss.

"Babe, you are making things rise up down there."

"Who? Me? Never. I'm an angel."

"A naughty angel in the nicest way possible."

"Babe, fuck me, please?"

Without hesitation, he was inside me.

I roll us over and am on top of him. He is holding my hips and grabs my breast.

"You're so sexy."

I glance down at him and his eyes are rolling back in his head. I know it won't be long now before his release so I do a hoola-hoop motion a couple of times and that's all it takes. He is saying my name as he climaxes. It isn't long before I find my release.

I collapse on his chest and listen to his heavy breathing while he runs his hands down my spine, sending chills down my body.

He whispers, "I know you're hiding something babe, but I am going to trust you."

I act like I don't hear him and calm my breathing. It doesn't take long before I'm asleep.

CHAPTER TWELVE
Time for a Lesson

"The best road to progress is freedom's road."
~John F. Kennedy

I can't say I ever really fell asleep. It was more like I dozed on and off throughout the night. Garrett on the other hand was sleeping—his snoring was his giveaway but I can't say I mind because he looks so peaceful when he sleeps.

I get up at four-thirty and get dressed. I walk over to the patio doors and check the weather. I open it, and can feel the cool rush past my legs and the rain pelts off the patio. This is perfect. The weather will wash away all evidence. I glance around and see a black vehicle parked down the street from my house. I know who it is, but I'm going to act like I don't see him. In order for this plan to work, I need to act normal.

I quietly leave the room and go wake up VI. Just as I raise my fist to knock on the door, it opens. I stifle a scream and put my hand over my mouth and on my heart.

"You bitch! You scared the shit out of me."

"Sorry Kay, I didn't mean to."

I whisper in her ear that Elijah is parked in a black vehicle down the road. She taps her purse, and I shake my head.

"Come on, let's go get Starbucks."

We gather our stuff, and I see a light on in the living room. We walk over and see Rodney there.

"You girls really are going, I see."

"Yes," we say in unison.

"Well, since I can't stop you, I want you to take this can of mace."

"Thanks Rodney." I grab it and stuff it inside my purse. "Take care of the house for me while I'm gone. I have tons of presents to buy. Oh, be ready to unload my truck when we get back."

"Oh great! Really? I get the joys of being the muscle?"

"You're the one playing house with my mom, so yes sir, you do."

That gets a laugh out of him, and we walk to the door.

When we walk out to the beast, I quickly unarm it and we jump inside. I turn the heat on, and VI turns the seat warmers on. It doesn't take long before the truck is a perfect temperature, so I throw it into reverse and back out.

We get out on the road, and I get a text stating Damon is in Seattle.

I hit the automatic dial on the wheel, and Damon answers.

"Birmingham, where are you?"

"I am just now leaving the house, but we have company following us."

"Oh damn! He's a quick one, isn't he?"

"You have no idea."

"Okay, so I did my homework on him. He has a temper, correct?"

"Oh yes, very much so, and his temper is going to be off the charts today. His brother is dead, and it's my fault."

"Okay, so what is the plan?"

"I was going to drop VI off at the mall, but seeing how I have company, she's going to have to ride along. I didn't want her to be part of this, but it looks like I can't prevent that."

"I know where there's an abandoned warehouse." VI says. "It's actually condemned and due for demolition this week."

"Okay, can you give me the address? That's where we'll make the magic happen."

"Perfect, we're only about a block from there." Damon says.

"Us too. I'm going to pull in and get out of the car. That is when I want your guys to grab him. Then VI and I will leave, and you can do whatever you're going to do. Remember, I want him alive. I want the last face he sees to be mine."

"Done. Not a problem."

"We're pulling in now."

"We're here but hidden, so come on in."

I look over to VI and tell her I love her.

"I love you too, Kay. Now let's get this fucking bastard."

We step out of the beast at the same time. I walk to the back and see the black car pull in right behind me. A chill runs down my spine.

He opens the door and says, "Superstar, you've been a naughty girl, and you need to be punished."

"Why are you following me? I know the police told you to stay away from me."

He moves closer to me and grabs my face.

"You fucking bitch! You killed my brother. Did you actually think I'd stay away? Oh, look! You've brought me a play toy."

"Leave her alone you bastard!"

I feel a sting across my cheek and taste the metallic taste of blood.

"You fucking dick! I can't believe you hit her. Have you lost your fucking mind? Didn't your daddy teach you to keep your hands to yourself? Oh that's right, you don't know your real dad, do you?"

That got her face slapped and before I know what is happening men come out of hiding and grab Elijah. They have a black sack over his head.

I hear him scream, "You set me up, you fucking whore, and I swear you will pay for this."

I look over at Damon who is smiling. I know he is going to have a good time because he can't stand rapists. His sister was raped.

I hold up six fingers, letting him know I will be back in six hours.

He shakes his head, and then Elijah is taken inside the warehouse.

VI is pulling me into the beast. She has the keys and throws me inside before placing the truck into drive and peeling out of the parking lot.

"Let's get the hell out of here."

"I agree VI. Let's go shopping."

"Wow! Really? We aren't even going to talk about him?"

"No we aren't. I want to go shopping. I have things to buy."

"Okay, where are we going first?"

"Well, let's start off at the mall because I might be able to get everything there instead of going to several places."

"Okay."

"VI?"

"Yeah?"

"Thank you."

"Girl, you know I got you. I wasn't going to let you do this on your own."

"I know and I'm thankful for that. I was scared shitless back there. He is just so unpredictable, but enough of the heavy. Let's go spend some money."

"Done."

We get to the mall in a few minutes and it's starting to rain hard outside.

"Hey VI, look! There is a parking spot right up front."

"Hell yes!"

She whips the beast into the parking spot. I take my purse and throw it over my chest sideways. She hits the alarm on the beast and we are walking arm and arm into the mall.

"So what all is on your list?"

"Well, I have to get something for everyone, but I know what I'm getting Garrett. I guess we can start there."

"Oh, what are you getting him?"

"I'm buying him a cross necklace. He has been trying with his faith lately and I want to get him something that could help."

"That's a great gift. He'll love it."

We end up getting everyone something at the jewelry store. I bought Patrice a beautiful ring that says mom on it. I got Rodney an engraved money clip. Wyatt got a sterling silver flask that says *Suck it, Buttercup*. And while VI was busy getting her gift to Wyatt, I got her a gold ring with two dolphins. She has mad love for them. I also ordered her a dolphin cruise on a glass bottom boat. She will get a day of pampering from head to toe.

"Kayla, there is a Christmas store right there. Let's go in."

"Okay, I want to do white lights with silver decorations and a splash of hot pink."

"I knew you were going to say that."

We walk into this store, and it's so beautiful. Everywhere you look there are Christmas ideas. Since I've never done the whole Christmas thing, I know my credit card is getting ready to have a major workout. I need everything.

I look around the store and see do it yourself gingerbread house, lights in every color, lights that play music, and there are candy canes, bells, and garland. I grab a few of the apple cinnamon broom sticks, stockings, and decorations.

I get candles and towels, and I look over and see an angel tree topper. It is gorgeous. She has blonde hair, green eyes, and a beautiful black and silver velvet dress. She also has silver wings and a halo. She is speaking to me and I know I have to have her. Looking around, I see a sales lady and I go ask for help, leaving VI to shop.

"How can I help you today?"

"I saw a tree topper that I am hoping is for sale."

"Well honey, you're in luck. Everything here is for sale. Can you tell me where it is?"

"Oh sure, it's right back here." We walk toward front of the store, and I stop where I thought the angel was. When I look up, it was gone.

"Honey, there is nothing there. Are you sure there was an angel on top?"

"Yes, but I guess someone else bought it."

I go back to the back where the registers are, and I tell them I'm ready.

"What's wrong, Kay?"

"I found the prettiest angel, and I went to get a lady to help me but when I came back, the angel was gone."

"Aww babe, I'm sorry. We can find another one."

"No, it's okay. I'll just make a tree topper out of ribbons."

I am waiting on the cashier to finish ringing up my load of decorations and I look down and see I have a text message from Damon.

It read, "Hey Birmingham, all is ready."

I reply "okay."

When the lady finally finishes, I see the smile on her face when she looks over at the total. It's seven hundred, sixty-four dollars.

"Holy shite Kayla! What did you buy?"

"Everything. I had nothing."

We gather all the bags and walk out the door as I tell VI it's time.

She nods her head, and we walk out to the beast, load our stuff, and get in.

"Kayla, what is the plan for Elijah? You mentioned a rig. I think I know what it is."

"Well, what is your guess?"

"Is a rig a needle? You use to shoot up, right?"

"Yes VI, that's correct."

"So what exactly are you going to do with a needle?"

"I've already told you I'm not telling you everything. If we get in trouble, I don't want you to go down for my stupidity."

"Kay, you're my ride or die. I'd do anything for you. I just need to know what's going on."

The guys grab Elijah and cover his face with a blacked out hooded cover. We have all worked together before so no words are needed. I give the motion for them to take him inside, where I have everything all ready.

***

I want to make Kayla proud, I have much love for her. I push this sorry bastard into a chair, and quickly my men have him tied down.

"Let me go you bastard, this has nothing to do with you."

"Oh but it does, you hurt my friend and now I am going to hurt you."

"Kayla is a whore, why in the fuck would you want to protect her. That stupid ass bitch got what she deserved."

"Oh really, you think I should force you to have sex? Tie you up and rape you? Take your ass and make it mine?"

I get the battery charger and touch the ends together. The sound of electricity makes Elijah jump.

"What was that?"

"Oh that is no concern of yours. I will show you what it is later."

"Why are you doing this? I have money, I will pay you whatever you want."

"Oh, you think I am doing this for the money?"

"Well, what other reason would you be doing this for?"

I rip the hooded cover off his eyes. It takes him a minute to adjust to the light.

"I am doing this because for years you and your stupid ass brother hurt my friend. I can't do anything with your brother because well, let's face it he is now worm dirt."

"You sorry mother fucker, I will kill you for talking about my brother like that."

"Oh you will kill me huh? I'd like to see you do that." I grab the clamps off the battery cables and I attach one to his left nipple.

I watch as his eyes get the size of softballs. And I turn on the charger. A jolt sends him convulsing in the chair.

"Tsk-tsk, looks like you have just pissed on yourself."

"I believe you guys used a belt of some sort on her as well correct."

He can't answer because the electricity is still flowing on a low dose to his nipple. I take out a black leather strap and I hit him on his chest. Immediately there are gashes.

I turn off the battery charger. And he vomits all over himself.

"You really are a sissy. I hear you guys tortured her for hours. And it was an on-going thing but I am not going to be doing this for long."

"What do you mean you are not going to do this for long, are you going let me go?"

"Oh no Elijah, there will be no letting you go but I won't be the one to kill you, Oh no Elijah that joy will lay with Kayla. She killed your brother, and now she is going to kill you as well."

"Please, let me go, I will never hurt her again. I swear."

"Too bad I don't fucking believe you." I slap him hard and hear his nose break.

"You mother fucker. You will pay for this."

"Oh please, you don't even know who I am. Kayla will be here soon and she will give you what you deserve but before that, I am going to show you how it feels to be tortured."

"She will never do it. I know that *Superstar* will save me."

"Funny how you think you know her. Guess what? She paid me to come out here. She paid me for the drugs that killed your brother, and she is paying me to fuck you like you did her."

I pull him out of the chair and throw him on the ground.

He tries to fight but it does him no good. My guys have him held down, and I have his jeans down around his ankles.

He is begging me.

"Beg please, god beg. I love it when a little bitch begs."

"I'm sorry, I don't know your name but please tell Kayla I am sorry. It was all my brother. He was the mastermind."

"Oh isn't that grand, you are blaming your dead brother. He can't even defend himself."

"I swear on my life that it was him."

"That is not what I hear."

I breathe in his ear. "I hear that you were worse than he was, that you took great pleasure in hurting Kayla. That it was you who also took great pleasure in raping her. That it was you who would beat her. That it was you, Elijah, that burned her with cigarettes."

And in one swift motion, I have him flipped around and I have my cigarette pressed against his neck.

He is breathing heavy and screaming each time I touch him with the cherry end of the cigarette.

"You thought I was going to rape you, didn't you? I am not like you, I don't have to rape someone to get them in bed, but I had your bitch ass scared shitless. You are no man, more like a little mouse." I flip the switch on high, and he screams in pain.

I knock him out and tell the goons to place him back in the car and make sure all traces are gone.

I send Kayla a message to tell her that he is ready.

***

It's pouring outside. I see the black car sitting on the side of the road. I tell VI to stay in the beast.

I get out and walk over to the car. He is bleeding and has bruises everywhere. Damn I see the cigarette burns along his collar bone and have to laugh because those bitches hurt.

I put a pair of latex gloves on and open his car door. He jumps at the sound and looks at me.

"*Superstar*, I knew you would save me, I told them that you would save me..."

I look at him with pure hatred, grab the rig, and drew back the syringe filling it with air. I move his neck so I can get to his carotid artery. I stab him suddenly and look out the window and see VI looking at me. I push the plunger, letting the air go into his vein.

He struggles, and I know he will die of an embolism.

I lean in close and tell him, "I am done being afraid of you. You can't hurt me any longer. Oh, say hello to your brother when you get to hell. Oh, the reason you didn't get raped wasn't because of me. I told him to do it, but you won't be so lucky because you are going to die. But I forgive you."

I walk away and never look back.

CHAPTER THIRTEEN
Meeting the Monster

"Life is really simple, but we insist on making it complicated."
~Confucius

When we get back inside the beast its quiet and I can see what had occurred is bothering VI.

"Are you okay?" I ask.

"Yeah, I'm fine. I never thought you had that much hatred. I saw the look on your face. You really hated him."

"He was a monster, VI. You have no idea the vile things he was capable of. For years he had a power over me and by holding that needle in his neck, I took back all that power. He can no longer hurt me or anyone else."

"I understand that Kayla, but I've never seen that look on you before. To be honest, it scared the shit out of me."

"I'm sorry, but in my defense I told you to stay in the truck."

"I know you did and I probably should have but I wanted to make sure if you needed help, I was there. I had my gun in my hand."

"Thank you for that, but I need to know if you can forget what you saw?"

"Yeah I can, but if you want me to forget, you need to tell me a few things first"

"Oh yeah? Like what?"

"Well first off, what did you do?"

"I filled his artery with air which will cause him to have an embolism."

"Okay, you are going to have dumb that down for me because I have no idea what the hell that is."

"I injected air into his artery that caused him to have a blockage. Basically I put a bubble of air into his blood supply."

"And how did you know you could do that?

I look over at her and see she is trying to figure things out.

"So what exactly are you asking VI? You know I am not just going to start talking about my past but I will answer if you ask the right questions."

"Okay, so when you were using, did you always use needles?"

"Sadly no. I snorted, smoked, and shot up."

"What is the difference? I know I sound like I'm an idiot, but I want to know."

"VI, I never thought you were an idiot babe, but I will tell you. Snorting is inhaling the powdered form of an illegal drug, especially cocaine, through the nose. I will give a run down on smoking Heroine. Heroin smokers start by attaining a rectangular aluminum foil about three centimeters by seventeen centimeters. You'll also require some kind of funnel tube to help you inhale the vapor. You can create one__"

"No! Stop! I don't need that many details. I understand," Vi interrupts me.

The look on her face makes me start crying.

"Oh Kay, please don't cry, I am just trying to figure things out, but I really don't need that much detail. I never plan on smoking the stuff."

"I know VI, it's just I looked at your face and you looked like you were disgusted. I am not proud of the path I took those years ago, but I did it and I have to own up to my mistakes. If I could do it all over again, I would but I can't. My past has made me who I am now. I am not shy about telling people I was a drug user. Hell, I will proudly tell anyone to not use drugs. Do you have any more questions?"

"Yes, how did you pay for your drugs?"

"I had money, but I didn't always use the best judgment when I was high. I slept with men for drugs. I traded sex for drugs. Hell I even stole for drugs. I am no angel," I say to her and hang my head.

"Oh Kay, I was not judging you I swear. I was just trying to get some background because the Kayla I saw a few minutes ago, I have never saw before."

"I never wanted you or anyone to know that side of me. This is my dark side. I've got the blood of Edwin on my hands, I have the blood of Elijah on my hands, and when I die, I will have to answer for my sins."

"Can I ask what it makes you feel?"

"I told you that if you ask I will answer. The euphoria of heroin is normally the first thing that hits you. The rush, coming up, whatever you want to call it."

"Can you break down snorting like you just did for smoking?"

"I can try."

"Here's what I can tell you about snorting Heroin or Black Tar. The first method, the one I call monkey water, is my preferred way. You put a bit of tar into a spoon as you would if you were prepping for IV. Then you add some hot water to the spoon, but not boiling hot. Hot water from the tap is more than adequate because it helps the tar dissolve easier. Next you mix it around in the spoon until all the tar is dissolved. I like to use a little piece of a straw to do the mixing, but it doesn't really matter what you use. Now you should end up with a spoonful of water ranging from dark brown to light orange. How dark it is will depend on how much tar and water you used."

"Now careful not to spill, bring the spoon up to your nose and snort a bit of the water. Do not try to snort the entire spoonful in one big sniff. If you do this, some of it will probably go down the back of your throat and/or just fall right back out of your nose and make a big mess. Snorting a liquid is a bit different than snorting powder, mainly because liquid doesn't stick to itself and every piece of moist tissue it comes in contact with. Also the liquid has much less resistance going up so you don't have to snort hard at all."

"The point being, what you want is it to cover your mucous membranes in your nose and sinuses. So do a little at a time until you get the hang of it. Sometimes what I would do immediately after snorting the "monkey water", is tilt my head forward so gravity helped move the solution towards my sinuses rather than just dripping out of my nose or down the back of my throat."

"If done correctly you will feel a mild burn and the onset of effects will be rapid. This method is extremely effective and not really very difficult to learn/execute. I just wanted to be detailed because I remember the first couple times I remember just railing it hard and having most of it go down the back of my throat and not getting me high lol.

"But anyway, this is the only way I did tar. In my honest opinion, the advantages of doing monkey water are it's fast to prep. You can get the dose accurate, there are no needles and track marks, and compared to snorting powder, it's a lot easier on the nose.

"The second method is called cheese. This is how you actually turn your heroin from tar into powder that can then be snorted. It's a bit more complicated than monkey water. The first thing you need is a surface to work on. You can use a plate, a mirror, a marble counter top, or a very smooth piece of plastic or glass. Really any flat, smooth, and non-porous surface will do. Wood is a no-no. I usually use a plate because it's easy to move around and clean up afterword.

"The second thing you want to do is make sure your plate is very clean and has no dents, chips, or cracks in it. If it does the tar is going to get stuck in them and it's a bitch to get it out. Also any residue on the plate is going to end up in your nose, and that's gross. If it all looks good then we can get started making our cheese. Now take your tar and place it on your plate. If the surface you're working on isn't very big try to place the tar close to the center so you have more room to work with."

"This next step is very important—"

"No! Stop! I've heard enough. I can't listen to this anymore. I understand now, and I know there's no fucking way I'd ever do that shit." Vi screams.

Now the look on her face is pure terror. I reach over and grab her hand. "This is why I never told you this stuff, Vi."

"No Kay, I wanted to know."

I look over at her and she is crying. I wipe away a tear because it's hard seeing your best friend cry. "VI, please don't cry. I can't handle seeing you upset."

"Kay, I am crying because you lived a whole life in seven years. I am so sorry that I was not there to help you"

"Oh VI, you could not have done anything. You would not have even liked me then. I was cold, had no life in my eyes. I did not care who I fucked over."

***

We sit in silence all the way until we get to the Christmas tree farm.

"Where are we?"

"I told you I didn't have a tree, so we're going to get one, and they'll deliver it tomorrow."

"Do you know what kind of tree you want?"

"I didn't know there was more than one kind."

"Oh, geez! There are all kinds."

We get out of the beast and start walking toward the lot of trees. I see a man dressed as Santa, and he is selling Christmas trees. I give a chuckle because I never believed in Santa.

"What are you laughing at?"

"Santa over there. I never had a present from Santa."

"Girl, you're killing me. What the hell did the Stanton's do for Christmas?"

"They gave us money. It was easier for them, and they didn't have to be home for that."

"That is so sad, but I understand why you wanted a huge blowout for Christmas. This is your first one."

"Yep, so let's get the biggest tree we can find. My ceilings are twenty feet high, so I think we need at least a twelve foot tree."

About that time, Santa walks over and tells us that he has the perfect tree for us. I look at him like he's crazy but who am I to judge? He walks us to the back of the lot, and there stands a tree so grand, it would put the tree at the White House to shame. I go up and touch the branches, and they're so soft. The tree has an amazing smell, and I know this is my tree.

"I'll take it!" I yell.

"Don't you want to know the price?"

"No I don't. I want this tree. Can you have it delivered tomorrow?"

"Ma'am, this tree is not cheap."

"Sir, with all due respect, I did not ask how much the tree was. I want this tree, and I am willing to pay whatever it is. I also need a tree stand. So when it is delivered tomorrow, please make sure they bring a stand that will hold it."

"I can see that I am not talking you out of this tree ma'am."

"No you aren't. So, let's ring it up. I'm exhausted."

I go and pay for the tree and the stand. He was talking like it was expensive, but it was only two hundred dollars—that included the stand.

"Come on, VI. I am exhausted and ready to get home and prop my feet up."

"Let's go, doll."

We make our way home, and by now, it's beginning to snow. I pull in to the garage, and VI and I grab a few bags before heading toward the elevator. To our surprise, Rodney is waiting.

"Are there more?"

"Oh, yes. The back of the beast is full."

I see him open the back, and I hold back a laugh.

"Holy shit, Kayla."

"We bought out the stores."

"I can see that."

"Come on. Grab what you can. I want to see them muscles work."

"I have them all, just hold the elevator."

"Okay," VI and I say in unison.

We get into the living room, and everyone is in there talking.

"Damn! Did you leave anything in the stores?" Wyatt asks.

"Nope, we bought it all."

"I'm just going to drop the bags and sit down for a few minutes because I'm dragging ass."

"Me too, Kayla. Me too."

As I drop the bags, Patrice's phone rings.

***

"Hello, this is Dr. Doyle. How can I help you?"

"Patrice, this is Seth, and I am not taking no for an answer. I will be at Kayla's in ten minutes, and we need to talk."

He hangs up the phone and Patrice looks over at me and says, "Kayla, Seth will be here in ten minutes. He says he wants to talk and is not taking no for an answer."

Rodney and Garrett both start talking.

"Fine, let him come in. I am sick of the damn phone calls, but I will not be threatened in my own home."

Within a few minutes, there's a knock on my door. Rodney goes and answers it.

"Officer Jernigan, what are you doing here?"

"That's none of your concern, but know that I will continue to be here."

"I just want to talk to my daughter."

"Come on Seth, we can talk in the office."

I walk towards the office and Patrice follows. All other eyes are looking at me like I've lost my mind.

"I'll be okay. There will be no problems, will there Seth?"

"No, Kayla there will not. I only want to talk."

I walk over and shut the office doors and tell them both to sit. I walk behind my desk and sit in my comfy chair.

"So, Seth, you wanted to talk. Now's your chance."

"First, I want to apologize to Kayla for letting the rape go on for as long as I did. I should have put a stop to it the moment I even suspected it. I should have kept you safe, but I was too caught up in my own life and political career. I am sorry."

"What are you sorry for? That you let it happen, or that you let it continue?" I ask, crying.

"Kayla, I am truly sorry."

He tries to come and hug me, but I push him away.

"Have you lost your fucking mind? Do you think I would let you console me? You're delusional."

He backs away with his hands in the air.

"Patrice, I owe you an apology as well. I never should have raped you, and I will spend the rest of my life trying to earn your forgiveness. I never meant to hurt you. I was not in my right mind that night. I was drunk."

"And that is an excuse!" I scream, "You raped someone. You forced yourself on someone, and you think that you can say *I'm sorry* and it'll be okay?"

"Kayla, I know you're angry, but I am still your father."

"Ha! That's funny. A father? A father is someone who makes you feel safe, kisses you when you're hurt, and tells you he loves you. A father protects you from harm. Did you ever do any of those?"

"I will never be able to take back what happened in the past. I was wrong. I hope one day you can forgive me."

"Are you done? Did you do what you came to do? Did you get it all off your chest? Is your conscience clear?"

"Patrice, can you please forgive me? I am sorry, and if I live a hundred years, you'll never know how sorry I am. But on the positive side—"

"What positive side? You raped my mother. You're a fucking monster!"

"The positive side is you were conceived."

"Good job! You created a child that you let get hurt for years. There was sexual, mental, and physical abuse inflicted by the hands of the kids you raised as your sons. Oh, but that's right, they aren't yours. So, is that why you're apologizing? You're trying to make things right? You can go since you've cleared your chest. I will never accept your apology. You'll never receive forgiveness from me. Go fuck yourself in the seventh circle of hell until you burn to ashes and are fucking dead."

I stand to leave, but he continues, "I understand that you have every right to feel that way and say those things, but I am truly sorry, Kayla."

"Don't come here feeding me some bullshit story just to make it easier for you to sleep at night. Guess what? It will never change the past, so stay the fuck away from me and leave me the fuck alone."

I turn to walk out, but I hear him say to Patrice, "I am sorry for what I did to you in college. Forcing myself on you despite the amount of alcohol is still no excuse. I'd like you to know that the regret and guilt of hurting you or letting Kayla be hurt haunts me and has for over twenty years. It will until the day I take my last breath."

"Well, that day can't come soon enough!" I scream and walk to the door.

Patrice is frozen and appears unable to speak, so I tell him.

"I think I speak for both of us when I say this. Seth, do the world a favor and just fucking kill yourself. You have no clue what you did. Let me tell you, you raped a woman. You took her choice away. All those years of you running for office, how would you have felt if the voters took your choice away? You'd have been pissed, but then again, you may have just swept it under the rug like you did with me. You treated me like I was no one, like I was a cheap trick. You sent me away Seth, with nothing more than a check. I had no one. I had nothing. Do you know I was addicted to drugs? Do you know I sold my soul to the devil? I was always looking over my shoulder. I was eighteen and alone. I have been fighting addiction since. I even bought drugs just the other day. Did you know that? No of course not. Do you know who stopped me from shooting up? It wasn't you. It was Rodney. A man who has known me for roughly a few months. He stopped me. He found me. Where the fuck were you? I am sure you were doing what you always do, you were probably balls deep in some whore who is young enough to be your daughter. Like it would matter to you. You have a thing for raping women."

"But now all of a sudden you are sorry. And I am supposed to just forgive you?? Ha-ha you got jokes. I will tell you when I walk out of this room, my conscious is clear. I have never wanted anyone out my life more than you. You have no soul. You will fit right in hell when you get there. You are a low-life bastard who don't deserve forgiveness. Make sure you tell your son hello for me. You are not worth me wasting another breath on. I am done with this conversation and I am done with you. After today don't contact me. Lose my number and forget where I live, because you are no longer welcome here. If I see you so much as breathing the same air as me, you better act like you have no clue who I am. I wouldn't spit on you if you were on fire."

I get in his face and tell him, "You are dead to me."

I walk out before he can see me break down. I will not give him the power to make me break, and he will never see me shed another tear.

CHAPTER FOURTEEN
Self Defense

"A life is not important except in the impact it
has on other lives."
~Jackie Robinson

I open the door and find exactly what I
expected—Garrett and Rodney standing there without
saying a word. I look at Garrett and walk into his arms.

"Did you guys get a good ear full?"

I can't be mad at them because I know they were
there to help if we needed it. The only person I'm truly
pissed at is Seth. I pull myself from Garrett's arms and
walk toward my room, closing the door behind me. I sit
down on the bed and cry. I know I should forgive Seth—
my faith tells me to, but right now, I can't.

I see Garrett walk into the room through my
watery eyes, and he sits on the bed beside me.

"Are you okay?"

I glare at him and say, "I'm not. He wants me to
forgive him, and I know I should, Garrett, but I can't.
These wounds are too deep."

"Do you want to talk about it?"

"Yes. I do."

He looks at me, his shock obvious. I can't blame
him for feeling this way because I always say no when
he offers.

"Where do I begin?"

"Wherever you're comfortable," he takes my
hand and raises it to his lips.

I wipe a tear that runs down my face before I
begin.

"All my life, the only thing I wanted was a family. I wanted a mom and dad. Well, now I have both, and I am so thankful Patrice has moved here fulltime and has started a practice. She's in love with Rodney and I couldn't be happier for her. I'm still hurt by the adoption admission, but I understand it better now. Patrice has opened her heart and life to me. She knows things about me no one will ever know and that's okay. I was hurt for a while when I found out she was my mom, but now it feels right. I can't imagine every having that bond with someone else. She is my mom, and I love her. Seth, however, is a different story. There is absolutely no connection or bond there."

"He had me my entire life. Hell, I lived under the same roof as my father all my life and he's a stranger to me. How is that for bullshit? I don't have the first clue about him. I couldn't tell you what he likes to eat, his birthday. Hell, I don't even know my grandparents. He never showed that side of himself. We didn't celebrate the holidays. The only reason I ever knew it was a birthday or holiday was because we all received money."

"But he sent me away like I was nothing. He gave me half a million dollars to leave. The whole time I was gone, if he had reached out to me, I could have saved myself from all the hurt I put myself through."

"I became addicted to heroin and sold myself for drugs. I did things I'm not proud of. I was constantly looking over my shoulder. When I finally got clean and sober, it was because of Patrice. She helped me see myself. The entire reason I am back home is because Patrice told me it was time. It was never Seth."

"Then I came home and all was good for six months. Then all hell broke loose. I got you all mixed up in this shit. All of you would have been better if I would have stayed away."

"Kay honey, I love you, and I am so glad you came back," he interrupts me.

"How can you love me after I told you what I've done?"

"Kayla, we all have a past we aren't happy with but you've made your life better. Your past only defines you if you allow it to. So, are you going to let it? I would love you no matter what you've done. You are my reason for breathing. I think of you before I make any decisions. I think of you before I think of myself. I would move oceans to make things easier for you. How can I not want to be with you?"

"I don't want the future to be ruined because of my past. Can you accept my flaws? I'm not perfect. I'm positive I'll fuck up more times than not but I will always stay on track as long as you believe in me."

"Kayla, I love you no matter what. One day I will marry you and then we are going to have beautiful babies together. I would ask you now, but I don't have a ring."

"Garrett, thank you for believing in me and remember I want a pink diamond when you ask."

He starts laughing.

"Can we get out of here for a little while? We can take a drive and see where we end up. I want away from all this fucked up shit."

A few minutes later, we leave in his truck and drive without saying a word for the longest time. He finally breaks the comfortable, peaceful silence.

"Hey Kay, that amazing band call *Last Moment* is performing at Club Fuchsia. I know you love their lead singer. Would you like to go?"

"Yes, I would absolutely love to go. I kind of have a mad crush on Alex the lead singer. She is a bad ass rocker chick. I know they made a brief appearance here last month just to check on the venue. I would love to actually listen to them sing. I am not really dressed to go out though." I am in jeans and sweater and thigh high boots.

"Kay, you could wear a wool sack and you would still be stunning."

"Aww, I know you are just trying to make me smile, but its sweet."

"Wyatt and VI are meeting us there. Is that okay?"

"Duh, I can't enjoy this without my number one Bitch."

"You really love her don't you?"

I look over at him and grab his hand, "Yes, I love her. She's part of my heart, the same as you and Wyatt."

I look out the window and see all the homes decorated for Christmas. I can't wait to get the house decorated.

"Garrett, I bought a Christmas tree today, and it'll be delivered tomorrow. Will you help me decorate it? I want to make this Christmas huge."

"I will help you with anything babe. All you have to do is ask."

Before long we are at the club, and the beat of the music is hypnotizing. I watch the people dance close to each other. There are people grinding on each other then there are those couples who act like no one else is around.

"Wyatt is doing well with this club." Garrett says.

"Yeah, he is. It was a much needed staple here in Seattle. Did he tell you he is thinking of doing a teen night on Wednesdays?"

"No he didn't but I think that would be a great thing to do. He would stay busy, and they need some place to hang out."

VI and Wyatt meet us and we party the night away. Toward the end of the night, I finally hear some good news. VI and Wyatt announce they are officially a couple, and they want to see where things can lead between them. Neither liked the idea of the other seeing someone else, so they made it *Facebook official.*

I laugh at this because I had given her shit about it just the other day. I have known they need it to just become exclusive. I can see the love they have for each other. It's about damn time they saw it and admitted it so they can see if they're meant to be—just like Garrett and I are meant to be. I mean, look at what we've been through, and we've made it work.

I raise my glass and make a toast, "It's about damn time you two finally saw what the world has seen for the last few months."

After, we all hit the dance floor and let loose, but before long I get an eerie feeling that something is off and something is going to happen, but I have no fucking clue what it could possibly be.

VI and I are on the dance floor while our men have a drink. We dance our asses off to the club-mix before *Last Moment* takes the stage.

I look over and see a woman walking toward Garrett. He tenses up.

I grab VI and tell her we have to get to the bar. She looks over and sees Reagan. The club is pretty packed, and the dance floor is where most seem to want to be. So we make our way over to the bar only to hear Garrett.

"You need to stay the fuck away from her. We're together now, and you have to fucking accept that and stay the fuck away."

I walk up with my biggest bitch face on and ask, "Is everything okay baby?" Then I kiss him with more raw passion than I planned but I really don't give a fuck.

So after we break the kiss and catch our breath, I turn to Reagan, "You need to leave."

"Oh Kayla, did you ever tell your precious Garrett what you and your friend here did to me in the parking lot last time we were all here?"

"No, I don't have to tell him everything. He trusts me, unlike you."

"Oh, so you don't think he would like to know that you and VI tased me and broke my nose."

I hear Garrett laugh.

"Are you seriously laughing Garrett? Your girlfriend messed up my face, and I have scars all down my body."

"Reagan I'm sorry, but your face was already messed up. I think I made some improvements. Now at least your nose is straight because before it was not. Your plastic surgeon needs some glasses." VI says.

I look shyly over at Garrett and he knows.

"I already knew. Wyatt has cameras you know. I have known since that night. We were in the office watching."

I look over at him stunned. He never said anything to me.

Wyatt walks over and tells her it's time to go.

"Here, let VI and I show you out." I say.

I take one arm, VI takes the other arm, and we drag her out the back entrance so I can share a few choice words with the cunt.

When we get out back, we let go and she start swinging and ranting, "You'll never make him happy. You're not good enough."

In order to shut her up, I pushed her backward, knowing her head will hit the brick wall behind her.

"Oh Kayla, you act like that was supposed to hurt. So I hit my head on a wall. Big deal."

"Reagan, I have dealt with your smart ass mouth since we were kids, but I am over it. I want you to leave my man alone."

"Awe, that is cute. You think he is your man."

"He is my man. He sleeps in my bed every night and is in my pussy every day." I see that I am pissing her off.

"Reagan, did you know that I make his eyes roll back in his head when I have his dick in my mouth."

"You are a fucking whore. First you sleep with your brothers, then you sleep with Garrett."

"I'm the whore? You're fucking hilarious. I'm not the one who got caught with two men fucking you in Garrett's home, and I heard that they had to have surgery. Awe poor guys, hope they are okay."

She spits in my face, and I slap her. "You fucking cunt. I am so over your petty childish games. You want to fight? Let's do it."

I have her pinned up against the wall and hit her face. I hear bones cracking. Blood is running down her face. I take a step back just to catch my breath and the next thing I know, I feel a knife slicing my hip. I reach my hand down and feel a slice going up to my ribs, and then I hear a gunshot. When I turn to look over at VI, she has tears running down her face. She keeps repeating it's over. VI is still holding her gun, and it's still aimed at Reagan's lifeless body on the ground.

"I had to. She would have killed you if I didn't stop her."

I walk over to VI, feeling the blood ooze out of my side and down my body. As I get to her, I take the gun out of her shaking hands and wrap her in my arms.

I whisper, "Thank you, VI. You saved my life."

I put the gun on safety and slip it back into her purse and call Rodney to come out. When he finally arrives, I explain to him what happened.

He agrees if VI had not taken action, the bitch would have tried to kill me or would have kept trying until she got the job done.

Rodney said he would be coming to write up the report and get everything all wrapped up in a nice neat lil bow and that he doesn't think any charges will be filled because there are witnesses to prove we did not start the fight.

By this time, the guys have pinned us out side and see a dead Reagan laying at our feet with a bullet hole in the center of her head and me bleeding.

So Wyatt locks the backdoor so that no one from the club can come out back.

Wyatt leads us to a bench, where he places thirty-two butterfly bandages on my hip and side after it had been cleaned.

I put my shirt back on, and Rodney walks in to take our statements, but no charges will be filed because VI shot Reagan to prevent her from killing me.

It was all caught on tape from the cameras monitoring the peer.

CHAPTER FIFTEEN
Forgiveness

"With the new day comes new strength and new
thoughts."
~Eleanor Roosevelt

We go home and have the most incredible
lovemaking session either of us has ever had. Afterward,
I am laying on Garrett's chest, and he has fallen asleep.
He always makes me feel so loved. I enjoy nothing more
than lying in his arm and thinking about how he took
me so loving but so passionately at the same time. He
has a way that makes me feel cherished. I know I am.

While I am having delicious thoughts of our
lovemaking and all the things he did to me, my damn
phone starts ringing and it doesn't stop. I don't want it
to wake Garrett, so I grab it from the nightstand and see
it's the police station calling.

"Hello?"

"Is this Kayla Ashby?"

"Yes."

"This is officer Jernigan's partner, Tracey
Mathews, and he has been trying to reach you all
morning. There's something you need to know. Please
hold."

"Hello, Kayla?"

"Yes, Rodney, what's going on?"

"Seth committed suicide early this morning—
around one."

"What? Seth is dead?"

"Yes, he was found by Millie. He was hanging
in the pool house by some purple ropes."

"Okay, why are you telling me? I wasn't there. I was at the club. You know that."

"Millie is saying she will kill you for this because it's your fault. Kayla, Seth is your father.

"Don't you dare say that vile man is my father? Yes we share the same DNA but that is all, he is nothing to me!"

"Kayla, I am not trying to make you have feelings for him. But the truth of the matter is Seth was your father. And as his next of kin we had no choice but to notify you. Millie is here screaming it's all your fault

"How is it my fault? I haven't been there in, well, fuck, since I left. I haven't stepped foot back in that house. So explain to me how this is my concern."

"Well, there was a letter addressed to you, and I'll bring you a copy so you can read it."

"His suicide note was written to me?"

"For the most part, but I'll explain more in an hour or so. I'm going to pick up Patrice because you'll need her shoulder when you read this."

"Why? I hated the guy. He never stopped the twins from raping me and when he was told about the abuse he just cut me a fat check to make me disappear. So, why the fuck would I care what he has to say?" I can't help but think of the last thing I said to him. I had told him that he was dead to me. I walk out of the room so not to wake Garrett. "Millie has said that she will kill you for this because it was your fault."

"Kayla sweetie, I agree, but you need to read the note."

"Okay, make it two hours, and you have a deal."

"Okay, two hours and we'll be there."

I walk back into the bedroom. Oh, God, what the hell have I done? I wished him dead, and now he was.

"Garrett honey, you have to wake up." I shove him.

"What? Is everything okay?"

"No, Seth has committed suicide."

"Kayla, this is not funny."

"Do you see me fucking laughing? Please get up. I need you to go with me."

"Go where?" He asks, throwing on a pair of jeans.

"Apparently there's a suicide note left for me. I wished him dead. Is this my fault?"

"No Kayla, only the weak kill themselves. This is not your fault. Now go get dressed, and I'll wake everyone."

I sit on the bed with my head in my hands. I can't believe he did this. Why would he kill himself and leave a note for me? My words were harsh.

"I killed my own father," I say sobbing then I realize I should say a prayer.

God our Father,

Your power brings us to birth, your providence guides our lives, and by your command we return to dust.

Lord, those who die still live in your presence, their lives change but do not end. I pray in hope for my family, relatives, and friends, and for all the dead known to you alone.

In company with Christ, Who died and now lives, may they rejoice in your kingdom, where all our tears are wiped away. Unite us together again in one family, to sing your praise forever and ever.

Amen.

I am crying over a man who knew I was being hurt. My thoughts go back to when I was younger. I do remember one occasion that I thought Seth was the coolest person ever.

I had just turned sixteen years old. I wanted to learn to drive. So I had went and asked Millie and of course she was too busy. She was planning some event for the Mayor's Ball or something like that. So I was walking back into the living room and Seth had asked me if I was okay?

"What difference does it make? I will be the only sixteen year old who doesn't know how to drive," I mumbled.

"You don't know how to drive? Kayla come on I will teach you." He grabs his keys and we go out to his blue B.M.W. He throws me the keys and says "Come on. I will teach you."

I am so excited that I scream and jump up and down.

I get in the car, and look over at him, because I have no clue what I am doing. He goes over a few rules, about checking my mirrors and adjusting my seat. He tells me to buckle my seat belt, so I do as I am told.

"Next you are going to stick the key in the ignition and turn the key."

I do as I am told, and the engine comes to life.

"Place your foot on the brake and then put the car into reverse. Slowly back out of the driveway and keep your hands in a ten and two position."

I back out of the driveway, and then he tells me to put the car in the drive position.

Again I do as I am told. Before long I am driving down the road. He tells me to make a right, and I do. I see the interstate up ahead, and I act like it is not a big thing. Before long I am driving down the coast of Seattle. We have the top off the car and we are having a good time. No talking, just listening to the radio and enjoying the drive. We stay gone for most of the day. He even buys me lunch that day. We had seafood at some little off the wall place on the water.

It doesn't take long and my room is buzzing with people. I am numb, and I don't even hear them talking to me. I know VI is getting me dressed. I don't even care that Wyatt is in here while I am changing. She pulls out some jeans and a black long sleeved shirt. She puts some mascara on my eyes, and a little blush because she says I am pale.

I get up, but I am on automatic. I don't know anything that is going on. I am being pulled into the vehicle, next thing I know we are at the last place I'd ever come to again.

I am about to have a nervous breakdown.

I feel Patrice grab my hand and walk with me.

We are greeted by cops.

The officer says, "I'm sorry, but this is for family only."

Patrice says, "This is his daughter."

The cop then asks for Rodney.

Rodney gives a nod, and I am taken back to the pool house.

All of a sudden old images of my rape comes flooding back.

"Time to pay the piper, sweetheart." His words circled the air and sent shivers up my arm, making me nauseous.

"Please don't." I couldn't get those words out of my mouth. It seemed like the cat caught my tongue.

Edwin then lit up a cigarette and puffed away, making smoke circles.

Gradually, I crawled to my knees and gathered all of my stuff. And before I knew it...

He clunked me in the back of my head with his fist. I tumbled over and peered at the water.

Like a caveman, he dragged me to the pool house. As soon as I was aware of my surroundings, I tried to fight him, but he was too strong. I couldn't do anything but dig my nails into him and claw at his eyes. He forced himself on top of me and burned my chest with his lit cigarette.

The burning tobacco cuts into my breast and created marks.

Every time I fought him, more marks showed.

"Stupid ass cunt." He slapped me so hard that I thought my teeth and eyeballs were going to pop out of my damn head. He continued to drag me on the red tile floors kicking and screaming, I tugged on my hair to release from his hold, but I lost momentum and dark red liquid flowed over my back, matching the tile on the floor.

I whimpered and cried. Hell, I even screamed the last time. He tossed me into the game room of the pool-house like I was yesterday's trash.

My limp body rolled. I laid on my back, stunned and mortified to what would happen next.

Edwin snapped my hair toward him and ripped it as he lifted me up. I felt like the roots were coming out of my head.

"Scream bitch, no one will help your ugly ass." He sneered.

"Stop it!" I stomped on his right foot.

"Ow, you fuckin bitch. You'll pay for that." His left hand smacked as his knuckles dented my cheeks. As blood seeps from the corner of my mouth, he then slams me into the wall. His hands wrapped around my throat. "Shut your fucking trap, you cock teaser."

"Edwin, enough!" Elijah's booming voice echoes through the hall.

"Please, Elijah," I shouted. "Help!"

Elijah strolled up to me, soothes my cheeks and grabs a hold of me.

"Edwin, get the rope cuffs," he bluntly said.

"Why do I have to get the damn cuffs?" Edwin asked as he swayed.

"Because I said so," Elijah's face was full of malice. "Now."

Edwin snagged a purple rope that had hoops at either end from one of the drawers where their father kept his sex toys.

"Please," I shouted and collapsed in Elijah's arms.

"Go ahead and scream bitch, we love it when you fight us," Edwin said as he grits his teeth. "Just so you know the more you scream... the harder things will be for you." His voice vibrates through his throat.

I can feel the tension from here, I'm about to have a nervous breakdown. I grab my chest and start breathing heavily.

"I can't do this. I can't be here."

"Kay, we are all here with you". Wyatt says

"You don't fucking understand I scream. I can't do this. I can't walk into the pool house."

"Kayla, I want you to look at me." Patrice stops us and she grabs my face. "You are not that little girl, you are a grown woman, and you can do this."

"I can't, Please don't make me go in there. I know they will be there and they will hurt me."

With her hands on my face she says "Kayla, remember you are a survivor you are not a victim. You left. And you know that Edwin is dead and Seth is dead too. Come on grab your big girl panties and let's go."

"I am a survivor I mumble."

"Good now, come on let's go because if you don't Millie wins. She already thinks this is your fault. Don't give her more reason to doubt you."

"She will not win. I will not let her."

I start to run out but Patrice takes my hand. "It will be okay, just breath."

"I can't do this. I can't be here."

"Yes, you can. You need to face this."

"Will you stay with me the entire time?"

"Yes, I will. I'll be right here the whole time, but we have to do this."

"Okay, just hold my hand."

"I will baby, I promise."

We get to the pool house and nothing has changed. The smell of the chlorine is still very strong. I look over and see him hanging in the hallway. I hear the other cop say that he suffered and it wasn't a quick death. I overheard that he choked to death.

I can see where the chair was just out of his reach.

The medical examiner said he would have heard the blood pounding in his ears as his heart beats harder—the adrenaline surges through his body. The thoughts swimming through his head would have been guilt, anguish, and pain until he faded into oblivion. The smell is horrid. Seth pissed and shit on himself.

I look over at his neck, and it is stretched and deformed. His tongue is black and protruding and his legs and feet are swollen from the blood pooling at the lowest point causing his legs and feet to look horribly bruised.

I gasp because I was not expecting this. I thought they would have him down and covered.

Rodney walks over and hands me an envelope.

I turn away and open the envelope, and I see a neatly written letter.

> To whomever finds this:
> My life was not taken by anyone else's hand
> Nor did it have to end, but the voices in my head
> The visions of my daughter's crying eyes and sorrowful cries because of my own boys
> Not in normal teases but in torture of a sexual nature. I can't stand the nightmares that I barely raised.
> What has been done will scar her for life
> But no one sees the pain she masks
> Her innocence in tatters.
> And I didn't do anything to help her
> I am the worst
> To see what I wanted to see in my boys
> And not know the hidden truth behind my angel's eyes
> I am worthless alive so these are my goodbyes.
> Kayla I want you to know **I am sorry**. I never meant to hurt you. I hope my death will make your life easier. I will not burden you. Just know that this will be my way of taking your pain away from you.
> Please forgive me. I love you my darling daughter.
> Sincerely,
> Dad

I am numb. I feel nothing—no hate, no revulsion, no forgiveness. I am simply numb. As I start to walk out of the room, everything goes black.

I wake up some time later with people around me, screaming. I lay still because I don't want to move. As long as I am not moving no one will know that I have woke up. I must have passed out.

Millie is now in the room, I can hear her yelling that I will pay for this.

Rodney then says we have more bad news. Elijah was found dead as well.

CHAPTER SIXTEEN

Letting the Past Go

"It's not stress that kills us, it is our reaction to it."
~Hans Selve

Millie comes charging at me, screaming curse words.

"This is all your fault. You are nothing. I knew you would end up taking everything away from me."

"What do you mean this is my fault? I have not stepped foot back in this God-forsaken house. I hated living here. I didn't kill Seth, and I damn sure didn't kill Elijah."

"Excuse me, but my husband is dead because of you. He told me what you said. You wished he was dead."

"Millie, I wish you were dead too, but it doesn't mean it would be my fault if you suddenly died."

"Kayla, I knew from the beginning you were Seth's daughter. Why do you think we got you? I knew about him raping your mother. Hell, I covered it up at the college."

"Are you insane? That's a dumb question. Of course you are. Why would you do that? How did you know about the rape?"

"Oh honey, I know about all the whores in the cock house. I know about every woman who my husband has let his cock play with."

"You're a sick bitch. Why didn't you ever tell him I was his? You could have prevented everything.

The rapes, the beatings, and the deaths. Have you lost your fucking mind?" I go after her and manage to get my hands around her throat. "You crazy, fucking cunt." I am squeezing her, and then I am pulled off.

She screams she wants me arrested.

"Go ahead and arrest me," I scream at her. "All of this is your fucking fault."

Rodney gets everyone out of the room other than the family.

"Millie, I want you to know you are the nastiest person I have ever met. Your husband rapes women, and you cover it up. Then your evil sons rape and torture an innocent child. You chose her because she was mine and Seth's. So because you couldn't have a biological child with Seth, you use ours. What kind of person does that? You need help. I hope that you get the help you need." Patrice screams at her.

"Millie, I hate to tell you this but you are under arrest." Rodney tells her.

"Me? Why am I under arrest?"

'Well, I will think of something to charge you with but right now, let's just say because you covered up a crime."

"Aren't you going to arrest Kayla?"

"I didn't see a crime. I saw you provoking her, and she lashed out at you. So I see that as self-defense."

"Kayla, I swear that you will get what is coming to you."

"Tsk-tsk. Oh Millie, you threatened her in front of a cop. Keep on talking. I am sure there are more charges to add." Rodney says.

"Garrett, I need to get the hell out of here. I've been here long enough."

"Okay honey, let's go."

We walk out of the room, and I watch as they load Seth into the coroner's van, and Millie in a patrol car.

"Babe, let's go home. I want to forget this day ever happened.

On the way home, Garrett is silent for a few minutes allowing me to gather my thoughts.

Finally I speak up.

"I knew as soon as I walked in that dad was dead. I could see that he had struggled. He died all alone. I was not there for him. How could I be so selfish? All he wanted was to be just a small part of my life, and what do I do, I tell him I wished he was dead. Garrett he hung himself with the purple ropes that held me down for years."

"It's an unnerving feeling, knowing that all I had to do was accept his apology. He tried to call me last night. I hit ignore, Garrett I hit ignore on my father's last phone call. How can I be such a monster?"

"Kay, you are not a monster you are human. He hurt you, and your instinct was to have nothing to do with him. I am so sorry sweetie. When my dad died, I felt a huge sigh of relief but to be honest I was hurt. Even though he hurt us for years, it was still hard. You always hurt in your heart when there is a death."

"This one will be harder on you because you walked in and saw him."

"I will never forgive myself for not telling him I forgive him. Now I will never have the chance."

Garrett leans over and takes my face in his strong hands, and tells me that he loves me, and that I forgive Seth, then he will know. He may not know in the physical world but in the spiritual world he will.

I place my hand in my hands and I cry silently, and say a silent prayer.

Lord, you invite all who are burdened to come to you. Allow your healing Hand to heal me. Touch my soul with your compassion for others; touch my heart with your courage and infinite Love for all; touch my mind with Your Wisdom, and may my mouth always proclaim your praise. Teach me to reach out to you in all my needs, and help me to lead others to you by my example. Most loving Heart of Jesus, bring me health in body and spirit that I may serve you with all my strength. Touch gently this life which you have created, now and forever.

Amen.

I want to go home. I am quiet the remainder of the way home. It is snowing outside and it's so peaceful. I feel a little flutter in my stomach and tell Garrett he has to pull over.

"Kay, it's snowing outside."

"I don't care, please pull over. I have my hand over my mouth."

He glides the truck to the edge of the street and before he comes to a complete stop I have the door open and I am getting sick.

He throws the truck in park and runs over and moves my hair out of the way.

"Is there anything I can do for you Kay?"

"No, just get in the truck. I don't want you to see me like this."

"Babe, I am not going anywhere. I will always help you whenever you need it."

I wipe my mouth with the back of my hand and go to lift my head and I am dizzy. I grab the side of the truck for balance.

Garrett picks me up and places me in the truck.

"Do you want me to call the doctor?"

"No I will be fine. It's just the stress of the day. I will be fine I just want to go home and decorate our house for Christmas. The tree should have been dropped off, and I want to enjoy the holidays."

"Okay honey."

We drive through Seattle, and I notice all the snow that has fallen since we have been at the house. The roads are slick, and I tell Garrett to be careful.

"It's just a little snow," he says.

We finally make it home and we slide into the garage. I hold on to the 'oh shit' handle and scream.

We get up the elevator and the biggest tree I have ever seen is there waiting on me. I call the guys in from the elevator shaft and tell them they have their work cut out for them.

"Damn Kayla, this tree is huge."

"I don't know if it will fit."

"Oh yes it will. I have twenty feet ceilings. This is a bet I'll win."

It takes them roughly an hour, but my tree is up and in the stand. My house smells like a forest, and I love it. During that hour I have all the end tables decorated. The mantle is done. The house is coming together nicely.

I go and grab the ladder so I can start decorating the tree.

I get the lights ready, and I have every strand blinking at different times.

"Kayla, are you really going to put all those lights on this tree?"

"Why yes I am Wyatt. And this tree is going to be the best tree ever."

Garrett walks in with hot chocolate.

"Oh honey, you are a life saver. I was craving that."

"I'm sorry, but did you say that you were craving something?" VI asks.

It's just a saying, but that makes me think. When was my last period?

VI sees the look on my face, and hers lights up.

"So Garrett, when are you going to make an honest woman out of my best friend?"

"What do you mean VI?"

"You know, put a ring on it." She says, doing her best Beyoncé move.

"Oh, I don't know. I am sure it will come soon."

"Don't scare him off VI. I like having him around."

"I don't think you could scare that man off if you tried."

"Let's get this tree decorated because I want to turn off all the lights and just sit and look at it."

"Wyatt or Rodney, will you please start a fire? Garrett, I need you to please get your fine ass on this ladder and start stringing the lights."

He does what I ask, and I am enjoying the view.

In no time we have the lights on the tree. It looks amazing. All you see are twinkling lights. There is not a dark spot on the tree. Everyone is having a good time. We are all sitting there making small talk while Christmas music is playing in the background. Before long the tree is decorated, and it is stunning.

"Hey, where is VI?" I ask.

"I don't know. I think she went to the bathroom."

I get up to go into the kitchen, and VI meets me.

"Kay your tree is missing something."

I look at it, but I have no clue what it's missing.

"Where is it missing something?" I ask.

"Close your eyes and stick out your hands."

"Hell no, you may have ice or something."

"I swear it's not ice."

"It's only because I love you that I will do what you ask, but it better not be anything that is going to scare me."

"Kay if it does, I give you permission to shred all my sexy bras."

Oh hell, this must be something because she is a sexy bra hoe. I close my eyes, and she leads me to the couch. I sit down, and I'm waiting. It seems like forever

"Okay Kay, you can open your eyes."

My eyes pop open, and I don't see anything.

"What am I looking at, the tree looks exactly the same?" Then slowly my eyes reach the top, and there she is. My angel is standing proud on my Christmas tree. I immediately start crying.

"You asshole, you knew I wanted her. Why didn't you tell me?"

"I saw her the other day, I knew you would fall in love with her. So I took you into that store. I had already bought and paid for it. When you went to the front of the store looking for the sales lady, I had it taken down and placed in a box. I wanted to give you something you wanted. And I knew you would want her."

I'm bawling now, "It's my first Christmas, and you just made it the best one ever. I freaking love you," I go and squeeze her.

She whispers in my ear, "There is a pregnancy test in my bathroom. Go use it."

I look at her stunned, but I nod my head.

"Hey guys, please excuse me for a few moments." I wipe my tears

I hear Garrett start to get up, but VI tells him to give me a few minutes. I hear their conversation, and they're making small talk.

I go get the pregnancy test from VI's bathroom and read the instructions. I pee on the stick and set it on the countertop. I can't tear my eyes away from it, and almost as soon as I lay it down, it shows I'm pregnant.

"Holy shit," I think to myself, "I'm going to be a mom. Oh, God, what will Garrett think? Will he be mad? Will he leave me?"

Of course I know the answers to all these questions, but I still can't help but think them. Before I leave the restroom I stick the pregnancy test inside a book. When I return to the living room, everyone is sitting around the tree, discussing their Christmas wish lists.

I know in my heart I have to forgive him, so I grab my journal and start writing. I am so hurt, the words spill out.

> *You did not know*
> *Hell no one did*
> *How could anyone know?*
> *I kept it all hidden*
> *Locked inside*
>
> *I ran away*
> *As soon as I could*
> *I hid from everything and everyone*
> *Not looking back*
> *Letting fear rule me*

I fought alone
The demons
That threatened to rip me apart
Running only masked
The reality
It never stopped
Any of the nightmares
From haunting me
Day and night

I reinvented myself though
I came back stronger
All of it
Made me
Who I am today
And now this

Why
Why couldn't you give us a chance?
You could have seen
How far I have come
We could have moved past all of this
Had an amazing future together

You robbed me of all of that
Reopened Pandora's Box
And left me
Left me to battle alone
Again
You selfish prick

It was not your fault
Damn it
Why couldn't you just talk to me?

Now you are gone
And here I am
Facing the demons
I thought
I had conquered

Time heals all
Or so they say
For me time only mends
The cracks of my broken soul
To truly be free
From all of this
I need to tell you

I forgive you
I forgive them
I forgive me
I am closing the door
I won't look back
I hope that peace finds you
Wherever you may be

I close my journal and walk into the bathroom and look in the mirror. I place my hands on my stomach and whisper, "I already love you."

I get in the bed because the day has been an emotional one. I lost the man who raised me, and then I find out I am carrying the love of my life's child. It isn't long before I fall into a sound sleep.

I wake up to the smell of someone cooking eggs, and I haul ass to the bathroom to toss my cookies. The smell is killing me. When I think I've emptied my stomach, I stand and wash my face and brush my teeth to hide the evidence.

I go downstairs, and see my family laughing and talking.

I hear Rodney in the office on the phone, and I walk in there to check on him.

"Hey Rodney, what's up?"

"Well, Millie made bond and she has a court date after the New Year. The coroner and the morgue called to ask if you had thoughts on what to do with Seth."

"Oh, wow. I didn't even think about what would happen, but shouldn't Millie make that decision?"

"No, the will was changed last month, and you are his next of kin."

"I have no idea what he would want. I think we should cremate him and have a small service."

"If that's what you want, I'll call them. I think it's a good idea because I know how hard it was for you to see him."

"Yes, it was hard. I won't lie. I've never had to make any decisions like this, so I hope they're right. Can you make all the arrangements for me, Rodney?"

"Yes Kayla, I can. I will ask your opinion each step of the way."

"Thank you for everything you do for me."

"You are so welcome. You are family, and we take care of our own."

"You are so right."

Over the next few days, Christmas is in full swing at my house. Somehow my living room has turned into Santa's drop off. There are so many presents under the tree that you can't even see the floor. I have never seen so many. There are gifts for everyone under the tree. All sizes and shapes. The stockings are full, the house smells amazing. We have thrown a couple of pine cones into the fire.

Before we know it, it's Christmas. I am so excited to give Garrett his gift. He has several, but I am most excited about the little thin box. Over the next couple of hours we have a fabulous dinner, with all the trimmings. Wyatt cooked this time. His ham was amazing. It had pineapple and cherries on top. He made ranch mashed potatoes, homemade gravy, fried green beans, and he made this mac and cheese that had seven different kinds of cheese. I was in heaven. I had three plates of food. I was starving. After dinner it's time for presents.

I have waited all my life to experience a feeling like I am feeling right now. The gifts are exchanged, and there is paper everywhere. I see everyone has a pile of gifts. I tell Garrett there is one present in the tree that he has to find.

"What do you mean there's a present in the tree?"

"Exactly what I said, doll, and look in the tree."

"Okay, let me see what we have here."

He gets up and searches all over the tree. I see him reach into the tree, and he pulls out a slender box. I get my phone ready.

"Babe, why do you have your phone out?"

"No reason. Just open your gift."

He slowly opens the box and the house is quiet. You could hear a pin drop. He opens the box, and I see him look down, then at me, and once more at the box.

"Is this what I think it is?"

"Well, it depends on what you think it is."

"I think this stick is telling me I'm going to be a daddy."

"Would you be okay if that is what it's saying?"

"Kayla, I'd be over the moon. So don't kid around with me, is this your way of telling me that we are going to be parents?"

He comes over and grabs me and pulls me up. "Babe I am serious, are we going to be parents? Have you given me my greatest wish?"

"Well I didn't do it on my own."

Patrice jumps up and looks over her shoulder and screams, "I'm going to be a grandma!"

"Yes babe that is what it is. We're going to be parents. Are you okay with this?"

His silence makes me cry.

"No honey, please don't cry. I'm excited. I've always wanted kids and now you're giving me a child."

He scoops me into his arms and kisses me.

"And you said I gave you the best present. VI says"

"Your present was second best to the present I just got"

Garrett is kissing and tears are running down my face.

We hear, "Hey now, that's how you got pregnant."

We start laughing, and I am still crying.

"Babe, why are you crying?"

"I'm so happy. Are you still going to love me when I'm fat?"

"Honey, I can't wait to see your round belly. I will love you even when you are round because you are carrying my child.

"Garrett Winters you did not answer the question. I said are you going to love me when I am fat."

"I did answer, but I'd never call you fat. You could weigh a ton and I'd think you are perfect."

"I am far from perfect. I am Damaged and I have been Broken."

"Kay listen to me I will love you for a thousand years. I love you and it's because of your past. And yes you were Broken and you may be Damaged but you are fixing yourself. And even a broken girl can be fixed."

***

Before long Christmas is over, and it's New Year's Eve. Tonight is Wyatt's Masquerade Ball. Everyone is decked out. It is a black tie affair, but you have to have a mask. I ordered our masks around Thanksgiving.

My dress is a floor length with an open back. It had a slit on my thigh. You could just barely see the top of my garter. My hair is done to perfection, and so is my make-up. Of course VI dressed me. I have not started to show yet, I don't even know how far along I am. Wyatt has ordered all bar staff to make sure there is non-alcoholic drinks for me, which is fine because that means I can drink all the cute girlie drinks because they all come non-alcoholic.

Garrett is wearing a kick-ass patterned black and white mask and is dress in black like me.

VI has a purple mask that matches her purple and black dress, and Wyatt has on a half covering mask on his left side in a black grey tone. He has a purple shirt and black slacks.

He took tonight off to spend their first New Year's Eve as a couple and to celebrate that we are all back together and inseparable.

I am dancing with Garrett and we are next to VI and Wyatt who are also dancing to an oldie but goody, Mariah Carey *Always Be My Baby*. As we are dancing and being held close to our men, I finally feel that life is as it should be. For once things are going my way.

The next thing I know I am being ushered outside, and it is freezing cold.

Wyatt has the peer closed off, and I see why. There is a hot-air balloon on it. Garrett takes my hand and leads me to it. He helps me in, not saying much other than it's our first New Year's, and he thinks it should be our most memorable.

When we are settled in the balloon, I look at my watch and see it's eleven-fifty. We float high above the bay as the fireworks begin.

I turn in Garrett's arms right before midnight. I want to tell him how beautiful and breathtaking it is.

From up here, he drops to one knee and opens a ring box.

"Kayla, I have been in love with since the first night we spent in St. James. There has never been another that could compare to how I feel for you. Please make my lifelong dream a reality and say you will be my forever and always and that you will share your life with me. Will you be my once in a lifetime?"

I am speechless, and all I could do was nod my head with the biggest smile on my face. Our lips meet, and we hear the screams of midnight.

Yes, this year will be so much better than the past years of my life.

We land the balloon after a nice romantic ride down the bay to see the fireworks. By the time it lands, my family is there waiting to see the ring. I had not even looked at it until now, and I see it's a pink diamond like I wanted.

I am over the moon happy. For the first time in my life, I can say I am completely happy.

EPILOGUE

It has been a crazy few weeks. The holidays have come and gone. And my house is getting somewhat back to normal. Well as normal as it can be with all the construction going on. I wanted a big huge elaborate wedding, but with all the shit going on with the all the deaths. And never knowing what Millie was going to do. I told Garrett that we needed to just elope.

"Honey, it will be perfect no matter how we get married. As long as you are there, I will be fine."

He smiles and kisses my head. He has this look about him that says I am up to something, but I can't put my finger on it.

"Garrett, honey what are you up too?"

"Me, nothing." He says smiling at me.

I go about my business because right now I can't focus on him.

He hollers down the hall to be ready to go in an hour.

"An hour? Where are we going? And you know I need longer than an hour."

"I'm telling you to be ready in an hour. And I am not telling you."

I get up and go look in the mirror and do my make-up. I have no idea what he is planning so I go natural. I make an oval with my mouth and open my eyes to put on my mascara. My lashes are thick so it don't take much to make them stand out. I put on some light pink lip gloss. And just a smidge of blush.

I toss my make-up bag in my purse. I walk over to my closet, since he gave me no ideas of what we are doing, I grab a pair of skinny jeans and a sexy one shoulder top. I grab my six inch fuck me heels. I walk over to the dresser and grab a pair of the sexy panties that Garrett bought me for Christmas. These are white with light blue bows along the sides. I grab the matching bra. I spray some Wings perfume in the air and walk through. I get dressed and look in the mirror. I look over my shoulder and see Garrett standing there staring at me.

"See something you like big boy?"

"Oh yeah very much so? And I will explore it all later, but right now we have to go."

"Why are you rushing me?"

"No reason, other than we have plans. But you are not going to know about them."

I watch as he takes a blind fold out of his pockets.

"Excuse me. What are you doing?"

"Kay, have faith in me please. I want to surprise you and this is the only way I can do it."

"Oh I have faith in you Mr. Winters but I don't know about this surprise."

He grabs, my hand and kisses my knuckles.

"You will be fine, just listen to the sound of my voice."

"Okay, I will trust you but you better not do something that is going to scare me, because if that is the case we aren't having sex till the baby is born."

"Kayla I swear you will love it."

"I better."

He is guiding me through the house. I hear bags being gathered.

"Garrett, who all is here? I hear more than one person."

"Don't worry about it Kay, just listen for once in your life. No questions. Just enjoy."

He grabs my hand, and I know we are close to the front door, as I hear the alarm code being punched in.

Soon I am being placed in the beast and he says, "You need to wear the headphones as well. I want the music so loud I can hear it in the driver's seat."

He places the ear buds on my ears and immediately I am being blasted with Uptown Funk. I sit back and relax.

I feel him latch my seatbelt and start the engine.

We ease onto the road, and it don't take long and we are at our destination.

I feel him unlatch my seat belt. And he takes my music away.

"Can I take off the blind-fold now?"

"No, leave it on."

"Yes sir."

"I can get used to the sir stuff, ma'am."

"Yeah, well, if I don't like this surprise, you are going to get used to your hand."

"Dang Kay, that is harsh."

"No, you know I don't like to be scared. And there better not be anything that will jump out at me."

"Okay, I promise."

He takes me hand and leads me into a cool building. I smell candles and flowers, but I can't place my finger on where we are.

I feel the cool breeze as a door open. And then the mask is taken off my face. It takes a minute for my eyes to adjust. And when they do, I see I'm at St. James Church.

"Babe, what are we doing here?"

His face lights up and he says, "I know you said that we could elope, and you would be fine with that. But when we are old and gray I did not want you to have regrets. So I have planned everything. From the dress to your flowers."

"But how did you know?" I say crying.

"Honey, I know you. I know that yes, you would have been okay with quick wedding, but deep down you would have regretted not having the whole church wedding, so Vi and Patrice have been planning this since before Christmas."

"Are you fucking serious? How did you all plan this?"

"I have connections. Now go in that room and get ready. I will be the one at the end of the isle waiting on you."

***

I walk into the room and look at VI standing there.

"You asshole you knew."

"Yes, babe, I did, but I was sworn to not say anything."

"So, tell me what I am going to be wearing since you've picked everything out, ma'am."

"Your dress is over there, hanging on the hanger."

I walk over to the hanger and unzip the garment bag. I pull out a blush colored dress, and I gasp. It is the dress I looked at over Thanksgiving when I ordered the masks for the ball.

This dress is stunning. It is a ball-gown style dress. It has a fitted bodice that comes in at the waist and then flares out to a full, floor-length skirt with lots of volume for a more formal and traditional bridal look. I also have a Tiara. That has pink diamonds all over. I see I also have a pair of what look to be pink glass slippers.

My flower bouquet is what I pictured in my head. It is called La Vie en Rose Bouquet. Tiny butter-yellow tea roses provide the perfect foil for the myriad shades of pink found in these garden roses, spidery jasmine buds, and scabiosas with their pincushion centers.

I get into the dress with VI's help. She does my hair in a fancy up-do with wisps of hair hanging down.

"Vi, will you ask Patrice to come in here for a minute?"

"Sure, babe. I'll be right back."

I am looking at myself in the mirror, and I see my mom walk in. She looks beautiful. She has on a light pink formal dress. She looks like a million bucks. I have never seen her so stunning.

"Awe, baby, you look gorgeous."

"Thank you, Mom. I don't know how you and Vi did it, but you have picked things out that were only in my mind."

"We know you, Kay, and we knew you would regret not having the church wedding."

"Thank you so much for doing this."

"It was no problem at all, sweetheart. We love you."

"I love you all so much. Do you think Rodney would walk me down the aisle?"

"I think he would be honored."

"Actually, I want you both to walk me down the aisle, if that's okay."

"Oh baby, you made my life complete. Thank you for accepting me as your mom."

"I couldn't ask for a better person to be my mom. I am sorry I was so hurt when I found out."

"It's in the past, Kay. You have a future to look forward to."

I wipe a tear off my face, and she comes and gives me my first hug as her as my mom.

"Ladies it's time." I hear Rodney say.

He walks in the door and gasps, "Kayla, you are so beautiful. Garrett is a lucky man."

"Rodney, will you please walk me down the aisle along with my mom?"

"Oh, Kay, I would love to. Thank you for asking me. You've made my night."

Before long the music starts and I know that is my cue. Vi is down the aisle in just a few minutes. They open the doors and my eyes are filled with tears. The church has never looked more beautiful.

With Rodney on my left side and my mom on the right they walk me down the aisle to A Thousand Years by Christina Perri. It don't take long and I see my soon to be groom standing there looking at me. He has a tear in his eye and he don't even bother to wipe it away.

"You look beautiful," he whispers.

The priest asks who gives this woman to this man.

Patrice and Rodney both say I do.

He gives my hand to Garrett, and I see Wyatt standing beside him.

I am crying as the priest is talking. I don't remember anything he said till he said it's time for the Vows.

"Garret, will you please tell Kayla what is in your heart?"

"I believe in you, the person you will grow to be and the couple we will be together. With my whole heart, I take you as my wife, acknowledging and accepting your faults and strengths, as you do mine. I promise to be faithful and supportive and to always make our family's love and happiness my priority. I will be yours in plenty and in want, in sickness and in health, in failure and in triumph. I will dream with you, celebrate with you and walk beside you through whatever our lives may bring. You are my person—my love and my life, today and always."

I wipe away the tears that are streaming down my face.

He gently reaches over and wipes a tear that I missed.

"Kayla, will you please tell Garrett what he means to you?"

"You have been my best friend, mentor, playmate, confidant, and my greatest challenge. But most importantly, you are the love of my life and you make me happier than I could ever imagine and more loved than I ever thought possible... You have made me a better person, as our love for one another is reflected in the way I live my life. So I am truly blessed to be a part of your life, which as of today becomes our life together. On this day, I give you my heart, my promise, that I will walk with you, hand in hand. Wherever our journey leads us, living, learning, loving together, forever."

And we don't even wait for him to pronounce us as husband and wife. He has me bent backwards and is kissing me like there is no tomorrow.

"Garrett you have made me the happiest person in the world."

I rub my belly.

***

I am now showing, as I am about five months along. Garrett says that I am beautiful. I tell him he is only saying that to get in my pants. He laughs and kisses my belly. He sings to my belly every night. I will wake up in the middle of the night, and he is talking to our peanut.

"Babe, I have news for you."

"Oh, yeah? What is it?"

"I bet I can still shock you."

"Let's see."

"We're having twins."

"Don't joke with me."

"Honey, I swear on all things pink, we're having two babies."

He scoops me up and kisses me. The kiss turn to raw passion.

"Babe, please make love to me."

"You don't have to ask me twice, but are you sure it's safe for the babies?"

"Yes it's safe. I asked the doctor."

I kiss down his neck and across his collar bone. I kiss down his stomach and lick the V in his hips. I unbutton his jeans and his cock jumps free into my hand. I slide my hands down his cock. I hear him hiss. He pushes me onto the bed. Starts at my feet and kisses all the way up my legs. Within seconds, he is inside me. He stops for just a minute to allow me to stretch to fit him. He starts slowly and it doesn't take long before my toes are curling, and I am screaming out his name. A few minutes later he is moaning my name as well.

He lays his head on my stomach and whispers, "Daddy loves you."

To my Readers:

I want to say thank you so much for taking the chance on a new author. For all of you who have a major addiction to books, thank you for supporting my work. I have the best job in the world, and you are the reason for that. So thank you for being the wonderful, book loving people that you are.

Thank you to my amazing fans who send me messages telling me that they love my story.

Thank you to the fellow authors who have paved the way for me to do what I love.

Thank you to the friends who have supported me when I thought I'd never finish.

And thank you to my family who have listened to my characters talk, or scream in some cases.

Thank you to Stephanie Stacker who I could not imagine my life with-out, you are an amazing person.

Thank you to Patrice and Morey Krumm for believing in me enough to start our little publishing company Scilicet.

Thank you to my amazing, wonderful, kick ass street team Layla's Ladies, you all are truly a class act.

Thank you to Lynn Palmer for believing in me and helping me.

Thank you Rachel A Olson for making the amazing cover for this and all my books.

Thank you to my best friend Jennifer Cook who will always be my Violet.

Crystal Lynn Booth thank you for helping me fluff my book. I can't wait to meet you.

Sarah Lively thank you for loving my work. It truly means the world to me.

Kim King I can't thank you enough for all you do for me. I could never repay you.

Jenni Crawford thank you for fixing my extra comma addiction.

Julie Mishler who writes kick ass poems thank you for giving me your words to put in my book.

To all readers young and old, thank you for loving to read as much as I love to write. I can't wait to take this journey with you all.

Much love,
Layla Stevens

The poem in this book belongs to Julie Mishler. Thank you so much for giving me your words. I love you to the moon and back.

You did not know

Hell no one did

How could anyone know?

I kept it all hidden

Locked inside I ran away

As soon as I could

I hid from everything and everyone

Not looking back

Letting fear rule me I fought alone

The demons

That threatened to rip me apart

Running only masked

The reality

It never stopped

Any of the nightmares

From haunting me

Day and night I reinvented myself though

I came back stronger

All of it

Made me

Who I am today

And now this Why

Why couldn't you give us a chance?

You could have seen

How far I have come

We could have moved past all of this

Had an amazing future together you robbed me of all of that

Reopened Pandora's Box

And left me

Left me to battle alone

Again

You selfish prick It was not your fault

Damn it

Why couldn't you just talk to me?

Now you are gone

And here I am

Facing the demons

I thought

I had conquered Time heals all

Or so they say

For me time only mends

The cracks of my broken soul

To truly be free

From all of this

I need to tell you I forgive you

I forgive them

I forgive me

I am closing the door

I won't look back

I hope that peace finds you

Wherever you may be

Once: A Collection of Sinfully Sexy and Twisted Tales
(Anthology): Tonight Only (Release-May 28, 2015)

Chapter One

"Every gift from a friend is a wish for your happiness."

~Richard Bach

Addyson McNyte

The ringtone of Meghan Trainor's- All about That Bass scared the shit out of me. I was not paying attention to my cell phone that broke through the silence of the quiet one bedroom loft apartment. It has an open floor plan with high vaulted ceilings. Clean and sleek lines go throughout. Stainless steel appliances that came with the space. It is furnished with black leather furniture, with glass tables and the 60-inch TV is mounted above the fireplace, and I love it here.

I was preparing for an evening out on the town in celebration of my new job as a police officer in the city of Albuquerque, New Mexico. I recently moved here from Topeka, Kansas and now my future is looking bright. So bright everyone around me will need sunglasses.

"Hello?"

"Hey hoe bag it's me, Jasmine, What are you doing tonight?"

"Hey bitch, I'm going out to celebrate. I feel the need to cut loose and let my hair down. Because for the last several months I have not been a real woman, more like a woman in drag."

"To celebrate what?" Jaz asked laughing.

"You'll never believe it, but I got the job that I have been training for. I am so feckin' excited!"

"Feckin' Really. He he you crack me up with your word feckin'."

"Bite me, ass, but yes, I sure did get my dream job. So, I'm going to check out this new bar at the end of Prospect Ave called "Bailed Out". I hear that this is the place to find all the local smexy men, and since I am single and ready to mingle I am going to dance my toned ass off."

"Awesome! I bet you're wearing your black and hot pink eight inch stilettos, huh?"

"Nope, just the sixes tonight. I don't want sore feet tomorrow for my first day at the station."

"Okay, well, I was wondering if you wanted to go with a group of us to the movies. But seeing how you are going out I may have to talk them into going out with you instead."

"Awe, thanks love bug for the invite, and I may catch up with you later, but first I'd really like to scope out this place. I hear they have kick ass drink specials and this may be the only night where I am not so damn tired from working, so I am going to take full advantage."

"No doll, I understand .We might meet you in a little bit. I'll call everyone and see what the ladies say. I'll send you a short text when I know what the ladies are wanting to do."

"Great doll face. Talk to you later!"

I pressed the end button and placed my pink phone beside the deep farm sink next to my brand new pink coach purse.

What can I say, I have expensive taste. I splurge on very few items, which consist of purses and shoes! I can walk into a shoe store and have an instant Shoegasm.

I look at myself in the big mirror and put the finishing touches on my hair and make-up. I stare at my reflection and think to myself damn the training has really made my body toned in all the right places.

My long, black hair cascades down in the back with beautiful bouncy waves, which makes my perfect olive complexion stand out even more.

I apply a touch more of bronzer so that my skin would shimmer in the strobe lights causing it to give off a radiant glow. I apply a thin layer of mascara to give my lashes that lush look and make my blue eyes sparkle, and then I go over my plump lips with a nice shade of red lip stain.

Satisfied with hair and make-up, I stand up and walk over to my over-crowded closet and take out a simple, yet sexy, silver barely there dress. I slide it over my curvaceous body in an attempt to remove the smallest of wrinkles.

I spray some perfume in the air and simply walk through it. Not letting the fragrance over power my natural essence.

I take one last look at myself in full length mirror and grin with satisfaction. I know I am a beautiful woman, some would even say I am conceited, and I am okay with that, I know I look good.

I am a confident woman and know that I have curves in all of the right places. So far, not many men can resist my charms—at least none that I know of. It was time to truly celebrate.

I have not had any intimate encounters in the past year and hell, my vibrator is getting its fair share of love but tonight I am looking for the real deal.

I have spent so much time studying for my exams and working out.

When I started in the academy, I had it in mind that I would graduate with high rankings in all departments, and guess what, I did!

Out of the 25 people who were in class with me I was the only female to pass, Hell, I even out scored some of the men.

And I know it chapped their asses that they were beat by a woman. I had a big ass grin on my face during graduation because I did it. So tonight I am going to live, no regrets!

My hope for the evening is not to find "Mr. Right" but I'm interested in finding "Mr. Right Now". I want a wam bam thank you mam type thing tonight.

Tonight I will be like a man, "I will fuck your brains out and then leave you wanting more." I whisper to myself.

I have too much going on career-wise right now and a relationship would totally ruin that. However, the heat pooling between my legs had other ideas.

So, I grab my purse, and slip on those six-inch-fuck-me-now stilettos, and head out the door.

I am not what you would consider a very tall woman. That is why the heels are a must, because being the 5'1 lady that I am I have to add something that makes the men grow hard.

My sexy as sin shoes always do the trick, I wear them with everything, and even in training I wore heels. They all thought I was insane, but I feckin love my heels.

I find that they add the height and command the respect that my attitude normally gives off with half of the effort.

I am determined to have a great night tonight and only a man who knows how to handle himself and how to handle me will do.

WORKS BY LAYLA STEVENS

Broken Love and Forever Bound – Book One

Damaged Love and Forever Bound – Book Two

Also coming this year

Searching for Love – Book Three {Novella}

Everlasting Love – Book Four {Novella}

Breaking Avery

Finding Finley

Forever Tripp

Teaching Kane

Terrani's Redemption

Unlucky N Love

Once: A Collection of Sinfully Sexy and Twisted Tales
(Anthology): Tonight Only (Release-May 28, 2015)

About the Author

I was born in Tulsa, Oklahoma but moved to Pensacola, Florida in 1996. I have a huge family who I shocked them when I told them I was writing my first book. I have had a love a reading since I was young. Reading has always been my escape. I can read and be a princess or a warrior. Reading for me was always something magical. And I hope to pass that on to you all.

I am blessed to be the mom of a little girl named Sage who is the light of my life. {I call her Olga, and she hates it} I did not give birth to her but I choose her.

I am blessed with great friends who have always had my back. I have a lot to learn in this world of writing but, so far I am enjoying the ride. I have a fantastic Four that are my true loves. No names will be mentioned as they know who they are. I Love you all very much. {I didn't included alters in that comment}.

I'm very opinionated and have no filter. I speak my mind without thinking of the consequences. Does this get me in Trouble? Yes it does every single day. But I will not change. I march to my own beat. My mom says that I can be a one man band.

I am always willing to help out anyone who is in need all you have to do is ask. I never knew that writing a book would show me so much about myself. I have learned so much in a short amount of time. And I can't wait to learn more.

Are you Stalking me? If your answer is no then you should.

www.tsu.co/Authorlayla/22142148

Instagram @authorlayla

Pintrest authorlayla

Google + Layla Stevens

Pizap Layla.stevens.author@gmail.com

Tumblir @authorlayla

Twitter @authorlayla

Email Layla.Stevens.author@gmail.com

Like page

https://www.facebook.com/pages/Layla-Stevens/697947530238039

Amazon page

http://www.amazon.com/Layla-Stevens/e/B00MRB0TTM/ref=ntt_athr_dp_pel_1

Buy Links Amazon

Us http://www.amazon.com/dp/B00MR3HQZ0

Goodreads

http://www.goodreads.com/book/show/18773845-
broken-love-and-forever-bound

Goodreads Damaged Love

https://www.goodreads.com/book/show/25089097-
damaged-love

Goodreads Anthology

https://www.goodreads.com/book/show/25439598-once-
a-collection-of-sinfully-sexy-and-twisted-tales

Plague

My new addiction http://plag.com/app/